EASY PREY

A John Rockne Mystery

DAN AMES

EASY PREY

A John Rockne Mystery

by

Dan Ames

FOREWORD

Do you want more killer crime fiction, along with the chance to win free books? Then sign up for the DAN AMES BOOK CLUB at

AuthorDanAmes.com

PRAISE FOR THE JOHN ROCKNE MYSTERY SERIES

Dan Ames' writing reminds me of the great thriller writers -- lean, mean, no nonsense prose that gets straight to the point and keeps you turning those pages."

  —*author Robert Gregory Browne*

"As gritty as the Detroit streets where it's set, DEAD WOOD grabs you early on and doesn't let go. As fine a a debut as you'll come across this year, maybe any year."

  -*author Tom Schreck*

"From its opening lines, Daniel S. Ames and his private eye novel DEAD WOOD recall early James Ellroy: a fresh attitude and voice and the heady rush of boundless yearning and ambition. Ames delivers a vivid evocation of time and place in a way that few debut authors achieve, nailing the essence of his chosen corner of high-tone Michigan. He also deftly dodges the pitfalls that make so much contemporary private detective fiction a mixed bag and nostalgia-freighted misfire. Ames' detective has family; he's steady. He's not another burned-out, booze-hound hanging on teeth and toenails to the world and smugly wallowing in his own ennui. This is the first new private eye novel in a long time that just swept me along for the ride. Ames is definitely one to watch."

-*Craig McDonald, Edgar-nominated author*

"**Dead Wood is a fast-paced, unpredictable mystery with an engaging narrator and a rich cast of original supporting characters.**"

-*New York Times bestselling author Thomas Perry*

"**In DEAD WOOD, Dan Ames pulls off a very difficult thing: he re-imagines what a hardboiled mystery can be, and does it with style, thrills and humor. This is the kind of book mystery readers are clamoring for, a fast-paced story with great heart and not a cliché to be found. DEAD WOOD is a hell of a book.**"

-*Amazon.com*

"**Dan Ames is a sensation among readers who love fast-paced thrillers.**"

-*Mystery Tribune*

"**A smart detective story stuffed with sharp prose and snappy one liners.**"

"Packed to the gills with hard-hitting action and a non-stop plot."
-Jacksonville News

"Cuts like a knife."
-Savannah Morning News

EASY PREY

by

Dan Ames

"He who does not trust enough...
... will not be trusted."
-Lao Tzu

"Three can keep a secret if two are dead."
-Benjamin Franklin

CHAPTER ONE

It was the kind of neighborhood where the rats outnumbered the humans. The grass was five feet tall, the homes still standing were abandoned, plundered by gangs and homeless people, and garbage was piled everywhere, both from illegal dumping and a sanitation department who had stopped making the rounds years ago.

Even they had given up on the city.

Hawks occasionally circled overhead, drawn by the vast number of rodents and other vermin darting in and out of overgrown bushes and dead trees whose branches had fallen and become enmeshed in the abundant ground cover. There were sporadic signs that the area had once been inhabited by human beings. A portable basketball hoop, tipped over, with its rim missing and a base cracked and scarred. A mattress, a charred laundry basket and a Chevy bumper dotted the ragged urban landscape.

Occasionally, a living human being entered the boundaries of one of Detroit's numerous no-man zones. A homeless guy looking for beer cans tossed from moving cars, a suburbanite who'd missed a turn or was looking for a place to buy heroin, or a kid on a bike, bored, checking out new territory.

It was one of those kids, a girl on a pink bike, who first spotted the Buick. She stopped in the middle of the street, fearless because there was rarely any traffic at all, and stared at the vehicle.

She had just turned ten years old a month ago, and the pink bike had been her big gift. She had even given it a moniker: Pinky.

It wasn't new, rather refurbished. Where the paint was thin she had been able to make out a faded green color. And the silver on her tire rims was a little too shiny. Not new, but new paint.

The ability to notice these tiny details was what caused her to stop and give the Buick a second look. First, the back window wasn't smashed in. There wasn't rust all over the bumper. And she could tell that the frame was correct, meaning it didn't lean from one side to the other, like most of the cars she'd seen abandoned in lots around the neighborhood.

The stickers on the back were weird, too. "Yale." What was a Yale, she wondered? Usually those stickers are for sports teams. Or maybe a college. She'd never heard of Yale. And the letters DYC. Those meant nothing to her. Don't You Care? Do Yourself Cake?

The girl looked around. There was no one else here, like always. She could vaguely hear the freeway a few blocks over. A dog barked, but that was far away. A deep bark, probably a pit bull. Everyone had pit bulls around here.

Her stomach rumbled and she realized she was hungry, suddenly remembering she was supposed to be home for dinner by now. She didn't see what the big deal was, dinner was never ready and it was usually her brother making another box of that awful mac 'n cheese. He usually didn't mix it right and there was powder at the bottom of her bowl.

Gross.

In the end, what won out over her fear wasn't curiosity, but greed. If someone had stolen the Buick and dumped it, there could be something inside they missed. Maybe a phone. She'd seen all the kids around her neighborhood with phones but she didn't have one.

The pink bike was walked to the curb. She put the kickstand down and stepped off the street.

The vehicle, she knew it was called an SUV, had been driven into a dirt alley between two houses.

Whoever had driven it in must not have known what they were doing. It was one of those unofficial paths people used, not a road at all. Maybe they'd gotten stuck? It had rained the day before and it might have been muddy when the dummy had pulled it in.

The girl decided to get it over with as fast as possible. She ran up to the side of the vehicle, raised up on her tiptoes and looked inside.

She recoiled as if the vehicle had given her an electric shock.

Her feet flew as she raced back to her bike, hopped on, and took off for her home.

Even as she pumped her pedals furiously, she also tried to block out the image of what she'd seen.

A face, turned blue.

With a rope around its neck.

CHAPTER TWO

"You're a goddamn loser," he slurred at me. "I know all about you. You're a goddamn piece of shit."

The drunk facing me was not a bad guy. And considering what he'd just said, I had to admit that maybe he was quite perceptive, too.

"Have you been talking to my family again?" I asked.

Adam Barnes leered at me from beneath his half-lidded eyes. He had on khakis, a dress shirt and a sport coat. A tie, unloosened, swung crazily beneath his chin. He looked like your average suburban father, except for his liver. That was more like your average drunk on skid row.

Adam's wife, Carrie Barnes, had hired me to follow him for a few days because she was convinced he was cheating on her. He was, but not with a woman. He was having a torrid affair with a hot little Swedish beauty named Absolut Vodka. Occasionally, he'd invite her over for an orgy with Jack Daniels.

Carrie had known her husband had a drinking problem, but my job was to find out if something else was going on. It wasn't, from what I could tell. It was a good old-fashioned addiction to whiskey old-fashioneds, among others.

I was glad to see that Adam still had his job, although I knew it was a huge step down from his previous gig. At one point, he had been the CEO of a major healthcare network, with an impressive compensation package. Now, he was basically a salesman shopping around ad space on healthcare-themed websites.

"...fuck at's pposed to mean?" he slurred.

"Just a joke," I said. "Now how about you hand me your keys and we'll get you home safe and sound?"

It was one of those things that sometimes happened. I tried not to get involved with someone I had put under surveillance. In fact, I had tailed Adam yesterday when he was drunk, but that had been when he was at a local Grosse Pointe bar, just a few blocks from his home. This time, he had gotten plastered at lunch and decided he wanted to pick his kids up from school. I had called Carrie but gotten her voicemail. There simply was no way in good conscience I could let Adam in his shitfaced state pick up his kids and drive them home. He could barely stand.

"Come on, I'll give you a ride home," I said. "Or take your kids home and you can drive yourself. Or get an Uber."

"You...leave my kids...kill you," he said. He stepped toward me and I glanced around. No one was watching. I saw his fist bunch up and I knew he was going to take a swing at me. I was hoping it would be a big wide looping punch.

It was.

He swung and it was like a slow-motion video. I leaned back a hair, let it pass by me and then threw a short right that landed right on the button. Adam went down like a sack of potatoes that had been distilled into potato vodka.

I glanced around again. No one had seen me hit him.

My phone rang and I saw it was Carrie so I answered, as I stepped over her husband's body to block any view of him.

"Can you pick the kids up from school?" I asked before she could even say hello. I bent down and fished the car keys out of Adam's pocket. I wanted to get him into my car before the school bell rang and his kids might have a chance to see him. No kid wants to see their Dad sprawled out on the street, three sheets to the wind.

Carrie told me she was only a minute away and could get the kids.

I dragged Adam toward my car, poured him into the passenger seat and then got around behind the steering wheel.

I would drive him to his house, wait until Carrie got the kids home and distracted them, and then I would dump Adam in the garage or something. My vote would be to drop him into the compost bin.

He moaned in the passenger seat and I looked at him.

"I won't make you buckle up," I said. Immediately my car smelled like a barroom floor. "Jeez, are you drinking booze or bathing in it?" I asked.

Adam responded by snoring.

I put the car in gear and drove down Kercheval to Kensington and pulled up a few houses down from Adam's house. The Barnes' current home was a step down from their previous abode, which had been a huge mansion along Lakeshore Drive. Now, they were renting a house that had once been a foreclosure. Carrie was a smart woman, and she had restarted her career as a marketing designer. I admired her loyalty and wondered how long she could hold on.

Adam stirred a bit, opened his eyes briefly and they flicked over at me before closing again.

"Loser," he said and then fell back asleep.

We reached the Barnes household without any more

commentary and about ten minutes later, Carrie pulled up into the driveway in her Volvo SUV and I watched as she and the kids, two girls, piled out of the car and went inside. Carrie paused at the door and I saw her look at my car and nod.

I reached over and pinched Adam's arm hard enough that he stirred.

"Ow!" he snarled at me.

I opened the door, got out and walked around to the passenger side. I opened it and Adam spilled out, barfing in the process. He puked all over my shoes and for a drunk guy, his aim seemed just fine.

"Shit," I said as I jumped back, but he had gotten me pretty thoroughly. The stench rose up to my nose and I tried to look on the bright side; it appeared he had drunk his lunch so there wasn't any food mixed into the mess.

I grabbed him and dragged him out of the car. He staggered to his feet and I half-carried him to the house.

The side door opened and Carrie looked at me. She was a finely boned blonde, with clear blue eyes that were imbued with a deep fatigue that didn't belong on her still youthful face. "Take him straight downstairs," she said.

I felt like throwing him down the stairs but I helped him down and saw a black leather couch. With a little shove I pushed him onto it.

Carrie was behind me. "He'll sleep for a long time," she said. "And then get up and probably start drinking again."

I didn't know what to say.

"There's a hose outside," she said, glancing at my legs and wincing.

It was a good offer that I accepted, spraying the regurgitation off my pants legs and shoes. Most of the smell seemed to dissipate as I walked back to the car and heard my shoes make squishing sounds with each step.

The phone rang in my pocket and I fished it out, glanced at the screen.

It was my sister, Ellen. Also known as the Grosse Pointe Chief of Police.

"What are you doing?" she asked.

"Just hosed a bunch of puke off my pants."

"Yours or someone else's?"

"Someone else's," I said.

"Good. Then get your ass over to this address I'm about to text you."

"Who died?" I said, joking.

The tone of her answer conveyed she wasn't in the mood.

"Your buddy," she said. "Dr. David Ingells."

CHAPTER THREE

Shit, there had to be some kind of mistake. *Dave Ingells?* Dave? The guy I'd done my first beer-soaked road trip with to northern Michigan where we'd ended up in a redneck bar and bragged about trapping beavers?

Dave, who'd approached Rhonda Bridgewater on my behalf to see if she had any interest in going to prom with me and who'd had to endure her explosion of laughter?

Dead?

Dave was dead?

He'd been one of my best friends before, during and after high school. He'd gone to the University of Chicago, eventually became a doctor and moved back to Grosse Pointe to become an orthopedic surgeon. One of the best in the state, even the country.

Car accident, I thought. Had to be a car accident.

I took a quick glance at the address Ellen had sent me, plugged it into my phone's map app and was surprised where Ellen was. It was in an area of Detroit not too far from Grosse Pointe, but one that was as desolate as the city can be.

It took me a quick ten minutes to get there and I knew I

was in the right place by the fleet of cop cars and bystanders milling around, some taking pictures with their phones.

It was another mostly abandoned part of Detroit, which seemed redundant but the city had been experiencing a resurgence recently. Still, there were huge tracts of land, largely vacant except for drug dealers and stray pit bulls.

The area bordered Grosse Pointe on the south and west.

A side street two blocks from the scene was a good place to stash my car. I parked there and walked toward the first cluster of cops I saw. Ellen was standing in the middle.

They all looked at me and the two cops on either side of my sister walked away. I had been a Grosse Pointe cop once, a long time ago. It hadn't ended well and I was still not a welcome sight for most of the squad. Playing a major role in disgracing the police department tended to not make you very popular.

"What the hell's going on?" I asked.

"It's not good, John," she said.

My sister Ellen was about my height, but thinner and tougher. She had the fine Rockne features, but with brown eyes and dark brown hair, unlike my blue-green eyes and slightly lighter hair color. People said they could instantly tell we were brother and sister, but I figured that was because we were so clearly opposites. In that, I was nice, and Ellen was mean.

"Yeah, I assumed it wasn't going to be a cakewalk when you told me my friend was dead." I looked around at the cops, the cars.

"This was no car accident," I pointed out.

"No, we're not exactly sure what it is," she said. "But it wasn't a car accident."

"Shit. Where is he?"

"On his way to the morgue."

Goddamnit. Dave was married. He had four kids. One

girl, living in New York. One boy at the University of Michigan. Two girls in high school.

Holy hell.

"What do you know?"

"Not much, and I hate to speculate," she said.

"Come on Ellen, it's me."

She looked at me. Even without makeup she was a looker. She'd always been beautiful, but once she became a cop she constantly downplayed her looks, for all of the obvious reasons.

"First guess would be strangulation," she said, ignoring her comment about speculating. "He had a rope around his neck."

"A rope?"

She grimaced. "Afraid so."

"Jesus Christ," I said. "A fucking rope. What the hell? Was he tied up? Arms and feet?"

"I don't believe so," she said.

I thought about that. "Auto eroticism?" I asked. I was reminded of the actor David Carradine, found hung to death in his hotel room. They claimed it was auto eroticism, which as I understand it, was the act of masturbating while severely limiting your oxygen intake. It was supposed to intensify an orgasm dramatically. If you didn't die, that is.

Ellen made a face like she'd bitten into something sour. "That would be odd," she said. "Drive out here? Pull into an alley? Put a rope around your neck and whack off?"

"Shit," I said. "Someone killed him. Drove him out here and dumped him."

My sister kept her face neutral, but I knew that was the basic conclusion she'd arrived at, too.

Suddenly, it dawned on me why Ellen had called.

"You want me to tell Christine, don't you?" I said. My

sister was a lot of things. But sweet and sentimental and thoughtful didn't apply.

She nodded. "Yeah. I have to go and tell her, but I figured you could do a lot of the hand-holding stuff since you know them a lot better than I do."

Ellen was my big sister, and hadn't known Dave as well as I had. Still, practically everyone in Grosse Pointe knew everyone else, to a certain extent. But she was right, I did know Christine fairly well and it would probably help if I was there when she found out.

"At least show me what you have," I said.

"Okay," Ellen responded. "Not much to show you really."

She led me over to the dirt and grass-covered alley between the two dilapidated buildings. I recognized Dave's Buick SUV immediately. It was the only one I knew that sported both a Yale window cling and a DYC sticker for Detroit Yacht Club. Even though Dave could have afforded a top-of-the-line import, he had always chosen to drive a Buick, supporting the idea of buying American.

"What the hell was he doing out here?" I said to Ellen.

"Nothing good, that's for sure," she said. "A Grosse Pointer out here isn't looking to be a community volunteer."

"Unless he was carjacked, forced to drive out here."

"We're looking into that possibility," she said. "This is as close as you can come," she said.

There were other cops, as well as a detective hovering nearby, writing in their notepads and working their phones. It wouldn't do for Ellen to allow a civilian too close to the crime scene. If she was accused of contaminating the scene, it would be bad news for her.

"Any broken windows?"

"No."

Car thieves loved to knock out rear windows which were less noticeable than the main front windows, especially driver's side. They usually knocked out all of the glass to make it even harder to tell if the window was just down, as opposed to smashed.

"Any calls from him about his car being stolen? 911?"

Ellen shook her head. "Nothing so far."

I looked around the crime scene. The tape went all the way around the Buick, but there was nothing but long grass and mud. Across the alley in one of the abandoned lots I saw some garbage. Maybe a plastic bag and a beer can or two. There were a few kids on bikes, slowly cruising around, checking out the cops.

"Who found him?"

"Young girl on a bike. She peeked inside and saw him. Probably have nightmares for a few weeks."

I didn't bother to ask if I could talk to her, I knew that wouldn't be allowed.

"We'll be done here in about a half hour," Ellen said. "If you've got time, I'd like you to come with me to talk to Dave's wife."

Dread filled my insides.

"Okay," I said. "I'll wait in my car."

CHAPTER FOUR

It was Ellen's job, so even though I knew Christine much better, professionally we had to have Ellen break the news. We pulled up one after the other in front of the Ingells' house, a sprawling Tudor on Devonshire Road, in the section between Jefferson Avenue and St. Paul, where the lots were the largest and spread out the most.

Point of entry for the typical house in these neighborhoods was around a million bucks or so, unless you could find a house owned by a little old lady who hadn't done any updates in thirty years. Then you could "steal" it for three-quarters of a million, if you were lucky.

Ellen parked her squad car and got out. I instantly knew the neighbors would all be peering out their windows and soon, it would be like a bomb went off once news of Dave's death started to circulate around Grosse Pointe. It was a tight community and word would travel like wildfire.

We didn't say anything as we made our way up the winding sidewalk. It was a cool evening and the chill in the air hinted at much colder weather on the way. Dave's yard was immaculate, with a neat boxwood hedge and matching topiary plants on either side of the front porch. Bluestone tile covered the cement porch, and a massive, curved wooden door greeted our arrival. Ellen pushed the lighted doorbell and we waited.

A cool wind picked up and rattled chimes in a neighbor's back yard and the faint sound was carried to us, a melodic jumble that perfectly captured the chaos of what was to come.

The sound of heels on tiles reached us and then the clacking sound of the lock being undone. The big door swung inward and Christine Ingells looked out at us.

Her family had come from South America a generation or two back and she was a dark beauty. Long black hair, slightly curled, an open face with gorgeous dark eyes. Full lips, perfect teeth and a casual elegance. It was easy to see why Dave had fallen so hard for her many years back.

When she saw me, she started to smile, but then a look of confusion came into her eyes as she registered Ellen's presence. Instantly, fear and anxiety took over.

"John, Ellen," she said. "What's wrong?"

"It's about Dave," Ellen said.

Christine sagged and I stepped in to catch her, but she put a hand out to the door frame and caught herself.

"What?"

I could tell Ellen wanted to come inside but she had to answer.

"I'm afraid he passed away, Christine," Ellen said.

Christine lost her balance and this time I caught her as she erupted in hysterical sobbing. I heard footsteps as someone came running down the stairs. I recognized the Ingells daughters, Valentina and Angie.

"Mom!"

They were dark-haired beauties like their mother,

Valentina a little lighter than Angie. Now, their eyes were wide as I helped Christine to her feet.

"What's wrong, Mr. Rockne?"

"Oh my God," Angie said. "Is it Dad?"

"I'm sorry," Ellen said. "There's been an accident. Your father passed away."

Now, the foyer was filled with tears and sobbing wails. Somehow, Ellen and I maneuvered the three into the living room on the big, soft couch and got them seated together. Christine was sobbing and trying to call someone on her phone. I figured she was calling her sister, who I knew lived only a few blocks away. Ellen went into the kitchen to put some water on the stove for tea.

Dave was a very successful doctor and his house reflected it. The rooms were enormous, the furnishings top of the line. The art on the walls reflected Christine's love of Mexico.

I held Christine after she finished sobbing into the phone to her sister. Somehow the girls seemed to be pulling themselves together, although they looked very much in shock. I knew they were in for a long process full of dark times and their lives had gone from carefree to a day-by-day existence that would never be the same.

On a side table to the left of the couch was a collection of photos from a recent trip the family had taken. They were all sporting snorkeling gear and sitting on the edge of a boat, clear blue Caribbean water behind them. It was hard to look at. I'd lost a friend, but they'd lost a husband and father.

Ellen came in with a tray of tea, looking totally out of place in her uniform and gunbelt. The sight of her started the girls crying all over again and Ellen gave me a look of helpless guilt.

Suddenly, the front door banged open and Christine's sister, Angela, raced into the living room. She threw herself at Christine and the girls and soon the four of them were hugging. Angela's husband, Todd, came in and closed the front door.

He was a physician as well and I was reminded of his always calm demeanor. It didn't fail here as he came directly to Ellen and myself.

"We've got more family on the way," he said. I knew that Christine had a large, extended family in the area, in addition to her sister. It seemed that the Ingells house was always full of food, fun and laughter.

I hoped that one day, it would be that way again.

Ellen and I both nodded, but I didn't envy what had to happen next. This was most likely a murder investigation and Ellen would need to ask Christine some questions. I saw her glance at me and decided to get it over with.

I walked to the couch. "Christine, do you think we could chat with you briefly in the kitchen? We just need to ask you a couple of really quick questions."

Christine nodded, and Angela helped her to her feet. I guided her by the elbow into the kitchen and sat her at the island on a tall chair. Ellen positioned herself next to her and I went around to the other side of the island.

"First, tell me what happened," she said, her voice a choking sob.

"We aren't sure, he was found in his car in a bad neighborhood in Detroit," Ellen said. Christine began to weep again. "I'm afraid that's all I can tell you."

Angela came and hovered behind Christine.

"Is this really necessary?" she asked, her voice had a sharp edge. "I mean, come on John," she said, looking at me. "Can't you do this later?"

"I'll keep this as quick as possible," Ellen said, before I could answer.

Christine nodded, wringing her hands. Angela glared at me.

"Had anything happened recently with Dave? Any reason someone would want to hurt him?"

The realization of what Ellen was asking hit Christine like a ton of bricks and she folded in on herself.

Her face was blurred with tears but finally she looked back up at myself and Ellen.

And then slowly, she nodded, yes.

CHAPTER FIVE

"It's not that there was someone who would want to hurt him," Christine said. "It's not like that."

Both Ellen and I waited while she sobbed some more. Her nose had really started going too and I wondered how much Kleenex they had in the house. I hoped they bought it at Costco, because then they would have enough to last several years.

Todd had now arrived and he stood next to Angela, both of them giving me the evil eye. Todd's was a bit more effective because he was one of those lean guys with muscles that made his veins pop out. He had a big one going on now, from his temple back into his hairline and it was throbbing. I felt its accusatory menace.

"It's just that there was an issue at the practice. With one of the docs," Christine said.

Ellen had her notepad and pen out. "What was the name of the doctor with whom there may have been a problem?"

It seemed like Christine had a hard time spitting out the name, but after some obvious internal struggle, she softly said, "Barry Kemp." It was barely a whisper, but I was sure I heard it right.

I knew Barry Kemp. In addition to being in the same medical practice as Dave, they'd also been fairly good friends outside of work. I seemed to recall several parties where Barry had been invited and attended. The image came to mind of a short, but muscular man with close-cropped gray hair.

"And what was the nature of the problem?" Ellen asked.

This time, there was no internal struggle at all.

Christine shrugged her shoulders. "I don't know. Dave didn't tell me."

The urge to glance at Ellen consumed me, but I fought it. I wanted to see if she knew that Christine was lying, because I sure did. The answer had come too quickly and too easily, even in her aggrieved state.

Which begged the question, why would she lie? And why now? Perhaps more importantly, how was she able to lie now? Having just found out her husband was dead. It made me reassess a few things I thought I knew about Christine Ingells.

Or was she really in a state of mind that allowed her to lie? Maybe I was just imagining things. She couldn't have been lying, and suddenly I felt like a big jerk for thinking so.

"I really think that's enough," Todd said. He was a good-looking guy, short blond hair just starting to go silver at the edges. He had a deep voice, with plenty of command.

And he was trying to use it now to get me to end the interview. But I knew I couldn't stop Ellen until she was done.

"Only another minute," I said. "I know it's hard but it's necessary."

A flood of reasons washed over me, but I knew it was pointless to try to judge their merit at this point.

"Even though you don't know the exact nature of the problem, do you know what Dave did about it?" Ellen asked. "Or do you know how big the problem was?"

If Ellen figured Christine was lying, she didn't show it.

Christine let out a deep, ragged sigh. Every time Ellen said her now-deceased husband's name, she visibly flinched.

Christine's face showed a moment of annoyance, as if she hated talking shop. "It wasn't a huge deal," she said, "but I know Dave had an issue with Barry and that it was important enough that they discussed Barry leaving the practice, which he eventually did."

"When you say eventually, do you mean it was a long, protracted process?" Ellen asked. "Were lawyers involved?"

"After," Christine said. "Once the decision had been made, Barry was gone and the lawyers got involved. Nothing went to court, but that's because Dave's lawyer is second-to-none. He protected Dave from Barry."

This brought Ellen's attention to the forefront.

"So Dave needed protecting from Barry?"

This time, Christine looked exasperated.

"Of course he did," she said. "Barry threatened to kill him."

CHAPTER SIX

In moments of rare lucidity, he knew it was the wine, not the mental illness. The question of which came first, the query his family members used to debate behind his back and then eventually right in front of him, had never been clear to him either. But that was because of rationalization.

In a movie he couldn't remember the name of, someone compared sex to rationalizing by saying it was much harder to go a full day without rationalizing.

Angelo Flores had done his fair share of making excuses. A bad day. A bad court case. A bad partner meeting. Eventually, they had grown to include a bad career, a bad marriage and eventually, a bad divorce.

So, he too had wondered what had come first.

Mental illness?

He'd always had a problem with depression, that was true. But a very mild, garden-variety.

But then the booze came along in the form of wine.

He had made the mistake of telling himself he was going to be a great wine connoisseur. It had always impressed him when men he knew could provide such detailed analysis of a wine they drank. The bouquet. The body. The different flavors. The origin of the grapes. It had all fascinated him. And, if he was being honest, it made him a little jealous. He'd felt a little stupid, even inept, when they spoke so authoritatively about wine.

So he'd begun to do his research.

Mostly by drinking.

Especially after a long day of practicing law.

He could get really intrigued by the different bottles he used to pick up on the way home. Sometimes, he would have three or four glasses at the store as samples.

Within a year, what he liked to call The Big Slide had happened. From wine, to liquor, to cocaine to heroin to homelessness.

It had taken more than a year, but within that fateful decision to get serious about drinking, he had lost it all. An investment portfolio that was nearing the one-million-dollar mark. A big house in Bloomfield Hills. Two cars, one of them a Jaguar.

To this. A bench in an empty park in downtown Detroit.

It had gotten cold, too, and former attorney Angelo Flores had a sweatshirt covered by a tattered Hugo Boss suit jacket. His jeans were filthy and his feet were encased in two pairs of socks and an old pair of high-top basketball shoes.

If only his old law partners could see him now. They actually had, come to think of it. A few months back a pair of them, decent guys, had come to see him, begged him to go to treatment.

He had refused.

Angelo Flores wanted no charity.

He just wanted heroin. Fast. Pure. Heavenly.

It was the only thing he lived for anymore.

Speaking of...

Angelo stood up and set off in a purposeful stride toward the Frank Murphy Hall of Justice. It was where plenty of lawyers still hung out and also drug dealers and the families of drug dealers. Sure, there were plenty of cops around but he had scored here many times.

And he needed it again.

As fate would have it, it was Angelo Flores's lucky day.

Within minutes, he had met a fellow junkie, but one in much better shape than him, with an unbelievable offer. In exchange for showing him a good place to shoot up, Angelo could have some of his dope.

With his skin crawling for a hit of the drugs that were now so close, Angelo quickly took the man to a building that had been in the process of being converted to lofts. Money had run out however, and renovations had stopped.

And Angelo had moved in.

He'd watched a man punch in the security code to the building, and had filed it away. Once he tested it and he'd gone in. There was no furniture, but there was a roof and some of the plumbing worked. The plastic sheets worked for bedding.

But best of all, it was a super safe place to shoot up.

He covered the keypad so his new friend couldn't see the code, and they both went inside. Angelo led him to a room on the first floor that had carpet installed.

They both took up seats on a pile of Tyvek wrap.

"Thanks, man," his buddy said. "I've been thinking about this for so long."

He shot up, then handed the needle and dope to Angelo who did what he'd been nearly tearing off his skin to do.

The last thing Angelo thought, as he began to nod off, was that his friend didn't seem to be affected by the heroin.

At all.

In fact, as Angelo's own eyes began to close the last thing he saw was his friend wearing a clear, happy smile.

CHAPTER SEVEN

My sister had never met a man who could stand up to her.

It was a pretty tall task, I had to admit. If I wasn't her brother, I'd probably be intimidated by her no-bullshit, gun-wearing presence. But since I was her brother, I knew the sly humor she often hid behind a gruff exterior. Oh, the humor wasn't there all that often, but when she unleashed it she could be funny as hell.

The fact that she was romantically liberated often meant she ended up at my house, hanging out with Anna and the girls, and out of necessity, me.

She actually followed me back to my house after we were done interviewing Christine Ingells.

Home was a modest colonial in a modest part of Grosse Pointe. Well away from Lake Shore Drive and its plethora of multi-million dollar homes. It was made with common brick and sported black shutters, white trim, a couple of nice white columns holding up the little roof over the front door and the landscaping always looked nice because Anna took care of that. If I was in charge of landscaping, there'd be mostly brown grass and a few dying plants.

I parked in the driveway because the garage held Anna's car and a bunch of furniture we were either going to reupholster, refinish, or recycle.

The back door to the house was up a short flight of stairs that led to the back porch, which was really quite small with just enough room for a couple of chairs. My grill was off to the right of the porch.

I unlocked the back door and Ellen followed me inside.

"Hello!" I called out and without waiting for a reply, went directly to the fridge and took out two bottles of beer. I cracked the tops and handed one to my sister.

"To Dave," I said and we both drank.

Anna walked into the kitchen and saw both of us.

"What's wrong?" she said.

I set my beer down on the counter and walked to her. "Dave Ingells died," I said. Anna's beautiful Italian face registered shock and surprise. She took a deep inhale of breath before letting it out. "What?" she said. "How?"

"We don't know," Ellen said from behind me. She walked over to the kitchen table, pulled out a chair and sat down. I joined her, and Anna did, too.

"Oh no, did you tell Christine?" Anna asked.

"Yes," I said.

"How is she doing?"

"About as badly as you would expect," I answered.

Ellen was checking her phone. "Shit," she said. "I gotta go." She pushed her unfinished beer across the table to me, but Anna snared it before I could grab it.

I knew better than to ask what Ellen had seen on her phone.

"Let's talk tomorrow," I said.

"Sorry I have to run, Anna," Ellen said. "And for leaving you here with him."

There was never an occasion where she couldn't rib her brother. I didn't mind.

"Take care," my wife said.

Once the back door closed, Anna turned to me. "Why don't you start at the beginning?"

So I filled her in on what I knew and what I'd seen at the crime scene, along with how Christine had reacted to the news.

"I'm glad she has so much family here," Anna said. "How awful."

Anna had gotten to know Dave and Christine fairly well. They were our friends. And I could tell she was struggling with the news.

"It doesn't change anything," I said. "But most of the time these kinds of things aren't random. There's more to what happened."

It was something that was never far away. When you shared a border with one of the most dangerous cities in the world, like Grosse Pointe did with Detroit, there was always fear that one day all hell would break loose. And it occasionally did. There were plenty of times a burglar from Detroit would decide to set up shop in Grosse Pointe. The problem was, Grosse Pointe's police department was really quite good. In no small part because of my sister.

"Oh God," Anna said. "This is going to be awful. I feel so sorry for the kids. I'll have to see if someone has setup a meal schedule. I can make them some lasagna."

We both took drinks from our beers. "We'll have to talk to the girls," I said. Even though our daughters were still young, they would probably need to be told about Dave's death, before they heard misinformation at school.

"Are you going to help Ellen?"

There was no doubt in my mind that this was going to be a murder investigation. But I had no idea if Ellen would want or need my help. Probably not on both counts. I had come in handy when it came to breaking the news to Christine, but that would probably be all of the involvement my sister would want me to have.

"Probably not," I said. "But—"

A strange, troubled look appeared on Anna's face.

"What?" I asked.

She shrugged her shoulders.

"It's nothing," she said. "Probably."

"Oh God," I said. Grosse Pointe was awful when it came to rumors. A small, tightly-knit community often generated a lot of gossip. "What have you heard?"

"You know Judy Platkin?" Anna asked quietly, as if someone was listening behind the couch. "She owns Village Toy?"

I searched my memory. I'd been to so many parties with Anna, mostly involving parents of our daughters' classmates that I sometimes had trouble remembering them.

Village Toy was the only toy store in Grosse Pointe proper. I'd been in there a couple of times, but it was really overpriced, even though they did have some hard-to-find stuff.

Judy Platkin? I tried to put a face to the name. Finally, I did. A tall, square-shouldered woman with a pretty, if some-what severe face. A brunette if I recall.

"I think so," I said. "Looks sort of like a pioneer woman?"

Anna nodded.

"What about her?" I asked.

Anna sighed. Finally, she spat it out.

"I heard Dave was diddling her."

"Diddling?" I asked.

"You know, sleeping with her," Anna said.

"No way."

"That's why I didn't tell you. I figured it was bullshit, and it probably was. Or is. Or whatever."

I had known Dave for the better part of twenty years. No way he was cheating on Christine.

"Who told you that?"

Anna shrugged her shoulders. "I don't remember. It was during a group coffee, I think Fran organized." Fran was Fran Daggett, a neighbor who lived just down the street. "Someone mentioned Judy Platkin and then someone else mentioned Dave being seen with her. You know Grosse Pointe. That's enough to get a rumor started. He was probably just shopping in the store."

I suddenly lost interest in my beer and I spent the rest of the night in a little bit of a fog. It was depressing. Not only was a good friend of mine gone, but I knew how Grosse Pointe operated. The rumors would start. Not that Anna was one of those kinds of people, but I knew there would be plenty of whispers. It made me wonder about how well you could really know anyone.

Dave had stuck with me through thick and thin. After I had been kicked off the police force for handing a young man back to his eventual killer, most of my friends wanted nothing to do with me.

Except for Dave.

Not only had he sought me out, I knew he had defended me as best he could. Of course, what I'd done had been indefensible, but still, I had appreciated his efforts.

Now, I had a chance to return the favor.

Something I intended to do until I had an answer.

CHAPTER EIGHT

I've always been an early riser. It started when my daughters were young. I would get up to do the early morning feeding and then I would just stay awake. After awhile, I found I had come to enjoy the silence of the morning, a house in which no one was stirring and a big cup of coffee in my hand. Some mornings I would work, others I would just sit and stare out the window.

This morning was one of my stare-out-the-window periods. I was thinking about Dave and how you never knew when, where or how the Grim Reaper might come to take you. He hadn't been the first in our friend group to pass away. There had been Brian Koshak, taken by prostate cancer. Another had been laid low by Lou Gehrig's disease.

But when someone your own age died, it created a jarring sensation. All of the canned expressions about not taking life for granted never did the experience justice. As I sat there, the steam from my coffee curling up in front of me, I vowed to extract every ounce of life I possibly could from every moment of my existence.

My cell phone buzzed and I glanced down. I had set it on

the armrest of the chair with the idea that it was pointless as no one was going to call me at this hour.

But I was wrong.

It was Ellen.

I slid my thumb on the screen to accept the call and raised the phone to my ear.

"Are you up early or did you never go to bed?" I asked her.

"Sleep is overrated," she answered. "Did I wake you up? Interrupt a sex dream involving you and Raquel Welch?"

"Raquel Welch?" I asked. "She's like seventy years old now."

"You've always had weird fetishes, John."

"I might need another cup of coffee to deal with this conversation."

I heard a ruffle of papers.

"Too bad. Here we go," she said. "Dave died of strangulation, plain and simple. No other signs of trauma to the body. No evidence of a struggle. No fingerprints, hairs or fibers."

"Wow, that's bad news," I said.

"Sometimes the absence of evidence is proof of something by itself," she pointed out.

True.

"Time of death?" I asked.

"Fairly safe to say he died Thursday night right around midnight."

"Had he been drinking?"

"No sign of alcohol or drugs."

I thought about what she was telling me.

"So you're saying someone strangled Dave and he didn't put up a fight even though he wasn't drunk or incapacitated?"

"He could've put up a fight, but he didn't have any marks on his body to indicate that."

"What about the rope around his neck?"

"No prints, garden variety rope."

"Shit, you've got a whole lotta nothing."

"Exactly. Nada."

"So what are you going to do?"

"We're still waiting for his cell phone records, which may give us a better idea of where he was or at least had been before he wound up in that alley."

My sister was really pushing the boundaries of acceptable sharing of information for the chief of police in a murder investigation.

"Is that why you're telling me this? You want me to share what I've found?"

I suddenly realized she had called me from her personal cell phone and she was probably at home, not the office. This was a totally off-the-record kind of conversation.

"Dave had a lot of friends here in Grosse Pointe, and they're putting a lot of pressure on the department to find out what happened," she admitted. "So yeah, if you've got anything, it would be helpful."

I filled her in on the rumor that Dave might have been diddling Judy Platkin.

"Diddling?" Ellen said. "What are you, a grandma?"

"I like the word diddle," I said. "It sounds fun and inno-cent, like a sweet childhood game of some sort."

"Oh Christ, why did I bring it up?" she said. "What about Judy Platkin?"

"Nothing about her related to Dave," she said. "Look, I gotta run. Try not to get yourself shot if you continue to look into this. You probably don't have life insurance and I can't pay for a funeral right now."

"Just put me in your garden," I said. "Every meal you'll think of me."

"You *are* a walking bag of fertilizer."

CHAPTER NINE

Like all small business owners, I worked far longer hours than your typical 9 to 5 cubicle monkey. What a horrible term. Although, to be honest, I felt a certain empathy for cubicle monkeys. Quite a few friends of mine had wound up in corporate America, trapped by a big mortgage and forced to keep the boss's butt clean.

It was part of the reason I'd become a cop, not wanting the dead-end corporate job. That hadn't worked out very well, though. Being a PI had its challenges, especially in the getting paid category. Sometimes it was feast or famine, but lately, I'd been doing just fine. I was happy, and Anna seemed happy.

That was all that mattered.

Anyway, Saturday morning found me making a big pancake breakfast for the girls. Isabel and Nina loved my pancakes – I poured the dough into the pan in custom shapes, mostly faces. It was like I was drawing freehand with pancake dough.

And then, since both of them had back-to-back piano

lessons that Anna always took them to, I used the opportunity to slip away into investigating my friend's murder.

The village was quiet on a Saturday morning, mostly people going to Starbucks or the bagel store for caffeine and carbs. There was a good name for a business. Caffeine & Carbs – full-bodied coffee with plenty of assorted bread products to go along with it. Screw all those low-carb people!

I made a mental note to suggest it to Anna. I'm sure it would be filed under Bad John Rockne Ideas.

It was a folder that was pretty thick.

My first stop was at Village Toy. It was a cute little toy store, full of most toys you could buy at Target for half the cost. They claimed to have hard-to-find stuff, but I'd been in here once when the girls were younger and left without buying anything.

Now, I pushed through the doors into the store and went to the cashier. She was a young woman, maybe even a high school student, wearing a Grosse Pointe South sweatshirt and yoga pants.

"Is Judy in?"

"Yes, I am," a voice said behind me.

There was an open doorway and the edge of a desk I hadn't noticed behind a tower of board games.

Judy Platkin stood in the doorway. She was probably in her mid-to-late thirties, with a wide, oval face framing two eyes the color of rich ebony. She was beautiful in a severe way, but her liberal use of lipstick plumped her lips and softened her appearance.

"John, isn't it?" she said. She stuck out a hand and I shook it. It was warm, with a strong grip that seemed to linger for a moment too long.

"Yes," I said, pulling my hand back. "Do you mind if I ask you a few questions?"

"Not at all, come in," she said. She walked behind her

desk and I took a moment to admire her figure. She had on a tight black skirt and her legs were encased in black nylons. A white blouse, also somewhat form-fitting, put her modest cleavage on full display.

It was odd because when I had met her previously, I'd remembered a rawboned woman who had seemed almost grim. Now, she seemed more curvaceous and was exuding a raw sexuality I found surprising.

"I'm sure you heard about Dave Ingells," I said.

"Yes, it was shocking."

Her face didn't show any surprise or deception. It was a blunt expression. Very open. Alluring even.

"Did you know Dave?" I asked.

"Not really, I mean we'd bumped into each other at a few parties here and there," she said. "You know how Grosse Pointe is."

"So nothing beyond that," I stated.

Her eyes narrowed ever so slightly. "Let me guess, you'd heard rumors I was sleeping with him."

I opened my mouth to deny it, but she stopped me.

"Oh, please. These bitches have gossiped about me for years out of jealousy. Just because I keep in shape, run a business, and their husbands hit on me constantly. It's never the man's fault. Blame the woman, right?"

I suddenly felt guilty being here. She seemed to be honest, and her anger was real. I just hoped she wasn't going to ask me if Anna had told me the rumor.

Luckily, she didn't.

"Look, I'm talking to a ton of people, because Dave was very well-liked," I explained. "I just want to know if you could shed light on anything unusual or surprising."

"No, we Grosse Pointers like to keep our sordid peccadillos behind closed doors, don't we?"

"We sure do," I said.

There really wasn't much more to say, because I knew exactly what she was talking about.

We made a little more small talk and then I thanked her for her time and left her there, in her little office, looking like a sexual dynamo and shrouded in a subtle but invigorating perfume.

My office was just down the street from the toy store, on the second floor of a building whose street-level resident was a high-end jewelry store. It sort of sucked walking past a store whose merchandise was absolutely off-limits in terms of affordability, then again, it kept me grounded. Hey, there were people who always had bigger, newer, shinier objects than you, right? Might as well get used to it.

Besides, I kind of liked having the jewelry store there. If it ever got robbed, I figured they'd have to hire me. I mean, I'm right here.

There was a staircase to the right of the entrance and I jogged up the steps, opened the door to the hallway, and then unlocked my door.

Rockne Investigations.

I'd paid good money for that sign.

Of course, it was tax-deductible, which is why I insisted on the best.

I unlocked the door and walked right into a fist.

The punch was off, thank God, and it missed my face, grazing my jawline before catching my ear.

There was enough force for me to stagger back off-balance, before everyone's favorite Grosse Pointe drunk, Adam Barnes, could follow up his lead-off punch. Now out in the hallway, I watched as Adam emerged from my office, his fists in front of him.

"You take another dime from my wife and it will be the last thing you ever do," he said to me. I smelled no booze, so I knew this wasn't drunk Adam. This was sober Adam, who'd probably just found out that his wife had hired me to follow him around and make sure he didn't kill himself or someone else.

"Does it matter that she just wanted to help you? And I was trying to help her do that?"

He let out a low laugh that sounded more like a bark. "We don't need your help. I know all about you, Rockne. You gave that kid up, right? Handed him right over so the guy could kill him? You're pathetic."

The words streamed out of him like pus from an infected wound. It didn't really bother me that much. I'd said far worse to myself about myself. And I'd heard it all before. In my line of work, you sometimes piss people off. And if they know you, know your background, they'll go there in a hurry.

I wasn't surprised Adam Barnes had dug up my past. He was desperate, not wanting to face himself. It was so much less painful for him to try to make me confront my own demons than for him to look at his own.

"Why are you here, Adam?" I asked.

Slowly, his hands dropped, but then he raised one with a finger extended that he jabbed at me through the air.

"Stay away from me," he said. "Stay away from Carrie."

He turned on his heel and walked to the stairwell from which I'd just come.

My ear was ringing as I walked into my office. I looked around, half-expecting to see some sign of angry Adam Barnes. Something smashed, or a puddle of piss somewhere.

But there wasn't anything.

He'd just waited for me. I looked at the lock on my door. No sign of forced entry, so how'd he get in?

What the hell.

Changing locks was expensive and I was going to be in no hurry to get it done. Still, it worried me a little to think of drunk Adam Barnes making frequent stops at my office.

I sank into my office chair and watched as my computer came to life.

Poor Dave, I thought. Without too much thought, I logged onto Facebook and checked his profile. It was still there. I desperately wanted to close it because the sight of those pictures, of Dave with his girls, was too much. But I had to see if there was anything there that didn't look right.

I scrolled past screen after screen of photos of Dave. There were no threatening messages, no sign that anything was wrong.

Then again, this was Facebook.

The epitome of superficial happiness. I heard it once described as an endless highlight film, because no one posted about how shitty their lives were.

I even took a quick look for Judy Platkin. Pictures of her with Dave, but of course there were none. It wasn't like if Dave was fooling around with her, he'd put a picture of them on his Facebook page.

That was enough of Facebook. I closed it and fired up Google, using it to search for Barry Kemp, the doctor in Dave's practice who'd apparently threatened him.

The only listings that came up were for him professionally. Doctor's grades, links to his medical practice, that sort of thing.

There was no doubt in my mind Ellen would be working on the case today. Murders of Grosse Pointers didn't happen all that often, she would be busting her ass to have this thing figured out. But I would need to stay out of her way.

Yet I couldn't help but realize that Ellen had been there when Christine had told us about Barry Kemp.

I drummed my fingers on my desk.

To meddle or not to meddle?

That was the question.

It wasn't exactly like Grosse Pointe had a huge police

force. If I just happened to have the address to Barry Kemp's office, it might actually be doing Ellen a favor if I went out and chatted with him. Heck, I'd seen that he specialized in orthopedics. I had plenty of aching bones. Chatting with him was a medical necessity.

Plus, I needed to see Barry Kemp face to face. He'd threatened Dave and now Dave was dead.

I wanted to see his face.

To see if there was murder in his eyes.

CHAPTER TEN

Before I could leave, Ellen appeared in my doorway.

"Have you been drinking?" she asked, sniffing with her nose. "At the office? Again?"

"Very funny," I said. "No, you just missed the husband of a client of mine. He's got a bit of a drinking problem and just suggested I not follow him around and protect him from himself."

She dropped into the chair across from me.

"Good. Let natural selection run its course," she said. I wondered why she had stopped by as we had just finished talking hours earlier.

"I tell you about the guy frozen to death down on Belle Isle?" she asked.

Belle Isle was a little island in the middle of the Detroit River. It had been the place rich white folks went to picnic on summer weekends. Then it had become a place for Detroiters to go. More recently, the state had taken it over and now that there was a fee to enter the park, it was once again becoming gentrified.

"Are you talking about Tim Flanders?"

Ellen nodded.

Tim Flanders had been a local man well known for his drinking problem. He used to drive down to Belle Isle, sit and get drunk. One night, he didn't come back. They found him a couple of days later in a stand of trees, frozen to death. No one knew why he had gone into the woods. Most speculated to take a piss. Others, too drunk to realize what he was doing. Maybe both.

"Your client's husband can either get help, or as the stock traders say, the market will correct itself."

I frowned. Kind of an odd way to put it.

"Why are you here, by the way?" I asked. "Needed to dispense some philosophy?"

"Dispense information, more like it," she replied. "Dave's cell phone records just came in."

She waited.

Finally, I did what she wanted. "And?"

"Seems he spent some time in downtown Detroit Thursday night. Right next to Wayne State's campus."

Wayne State was a highly respectable university in downtown Detroit. It was also right next to the midtown area of the city, which had recently become a lot more hip and trendy with cool bars and restaurants.

"What the fuck was he doing down there by himself?"

"Who says he was by himself?"

"Well, he wasn't with Christine. His wife. She would have mentioned they were downtown the night of his disappearance."

"Again, what makes you think he was alone?" my sister persisted.

"And what was he doing at Wayne State?"

"What makes you think he was on campus? Maybe he just parked nearby."

That actually made more sense. "So maybe he went down

there, was meeting a friend for drinks or dinner or something, and then he got carjacked," I hypothesized. "Someone forced him into the car, strangled him and then abandoned him."

My sister raised an eyebrow at me. "So they killed him but didn't take the car, his wallet or his TAG Heuer watch?"

"Okay," I admitted. "Doesn't make a lot of sense."

"Maybe he went to midtown to buy drugs and he ripped someone off so they killed him," Ellen offered.

"He wasn't on drugs. That's ridiculous."

"How about this, then?" my sister said. "Christine lured him to midtown, and hired someone to kill him. He's probably got a fairly big life insurance policy."

"They're already wealthy."

"You can never have too much money," Ellen said. She raised her hands. "Look, we toss out crazy scenarios left and right. You keep digging and let me know what you find."

She got to her feet. "Confidentially," she added. "I don't need anyone at the department knowing you're involved. There are a few people down there who still don't like the idea of having a female police chief."

"Assholes," I said.

"Yes, they are," she answered, her voice tired.

CHAPTER ELEVEN

A quick call to Barry Kemp's office told me he wasn't in today.

Hmm.

Maybe because his former partner and the man he threatened was just found murdered?

There were any number of ways to find out Kemp's home address. I chose the easiest one possible. I called my sister, even though we'd already chatted twice today. I was nearing the quota of how much time she would actually talk to me.

"Did you interview Barry Kemp yet?"

"What are you, my secretary?" she said. "I need to check in with you on my daily activities?"

"Nothing wrong with being a male secretary," I replied. "But really, I was just checking in on the case. See if you found anything out since we chatted a couple hours ago."

I heard her sigh. "John, I know I dragged you into this and I'm glad you were able to help me out breaking the news to Christine, but I can't be spilling a bunch of details to you. You know that."

"I know," I said. "Where does he live anyway?"

This time she laughed. "You want me to give you Barry Kemp's address so you can go and question him? Even after I just told you to butt out? You've got some cojones, brother."

"It could be useful," I said. "I can take the questioning in places you might not have wanted to go. I promise if I learn anything at all, you'll be the first to know. I swear."

"You never learn anything, John," she said.

But I felt my phone buzz, looked down and saw the text with an address, from Ellen's personal cell phone.

"Thanks—" I started to say but she had already disconnected.

Rude.

It was an address in Royal Oak, which kind of surprised me. Royal Oak was a young person's town, or a young family's town. Just north of Royal Oak was ritzy Birmingham, where I would have assumed the doctor was living. Maybe there was a section of Royal Oak on Birmingham's border that was home to the kind of residences a doctor might choose.

Or maybe Barry Kemp was young at heart and loved to hang out at bars with twenty-somethings. I had seen him a couple of times already at a party or two Dave had thrown, and I remember him as a bit of a fireplug, with short gray hair tinged with red that was almost a buzzcut.

I tried to picture Barry at bars in Royal Oak. Was he single? Gay? Divorced?

Only one way to find out.

With my phone's navigation app I drove from Grosse Pointe to Royal Oak via 696 and then headed north on famous Woodward Avenue. Woodward was where they had the dream cruise every year and the parade of classic cars went from the suburbs into the heart of downtown Detroit.

Eventually I found myself in a neighborhood of modest, but expensive-looking homes. Expensive mostly because the driveways were filled with Range Rovers and Porsches.

It was a Royal Oak neighborhood, but it had Birmingham written all over it.

Barry Kemp's place was a modern structure, concrete, glass and dark metal.

My car of choice these days was a white Honda Accord. I used to always drive gray sedans, feeling they blended in more than anything else. But now, I feel white cars are actually more generic, because of their association with rentals. People assume they're either rental cars or company cars, hence, they don't really take notice.

Kemp's front door was made of a dark, heavy wood and I used the metal knocker to announce my presence. I couldn't remember if I locked my car so I took out my keys and gave the remote a quick press to lock. When I turned back around, the door was open and Barry Kemp was looking at me.

"Barry?" I said, feeling more familiar with him than I'd thought I would be. But now I remembered that I'd actually chatted with him a few times at those parties of Dave's.

"John, right?" he replied.

"Rockne. John Rockne," I said.

He was short, wide and muscular. He was wearing workout shorts and a dry-fit T-shirt that showed off his bulging pecs and gorilla arms.

No doubt some serious overcompensation going on here, but it was impressive nonetheless. Proof that emotional focus could work wonders. I suddenly felt out of shape and flabby, even though I took fairly good care of myself.

"I just talked to your sister," he said. His voice smooth and eloquent, which surprised me. I half-expected some sort of gravelly baritone to match his physique. Then I remembered he was a doctor and had probably spent a lot of time perfecting his bedside manner.

"Sorry to hear that," I said. "I try to avoid talking to her as much as possible."

He sort of gave me a half-smile. "What can I do for you, John?" He remained standing in the doorway, his left hand holding the edge of the door, causing his bicep to pop. It looked like a softball wrapped in veiny skin.

"Well, you already know about Dave, I assume?" I asked. It was getting a little awkward not to be let into his house, but I wanted to play this right. I wanted to talk to him about what had happened.

"Yes, unfortunately," he said. "I heard last night from Todd."

Todd was Angela's husband, and Christine's brother-in-law. He'd been there when Ellen and I had broken the news.

Todd was a physician, too, albeit in a different practice. Both Angela and Christine, sisters, had married doctors. Dave had once mentioned that they had both been strongly urged as young girls by their parents to do so.

"Do you mind if I ask you a few questions?"

He looked pained as he considered his answer. "Is there really anything different from what I've already gone over?" Meaning, couldn't I just talk to my sister to find out what information had been gathered.

"With me, everything is off the record," I said. "Plus, I'm sure Ellen didn't tell you anything at all because she can't comment on a pending investigation. I, however, am a big blabbermouth and can share with you what I know."

He weighed what I was saying, and whether or not it was bullshit. Truthfully, it was mostly bullshit, but if I believed he was innocent I would tell him what I knew, which was jack shit.

Finally, he let out a long sigh.

"Come on in," he said.

CHAPTER TWELVE

The interior of Barry Kemp's home looked like it had been torn out of the pages of Architectural Digest. Especially if they were doing a special issue on modern styles. It looked less like a house than a museum of contemporary furniture.

I didn't know much about home furnishings, I've always been a fan of the La-Z-Boy line, but something told me that not only were Kemp's furnishings expensive, they were probably unique items. In other words, he hadn't run into the nearest furniture mall and unleashed his credit card.

"Something to drink?" he asked. "Coffee? Espresso? I have one of these machines I paid five grand for that I never use."

"No, that's okay," I said. "Coffee at this time of day would make me jittery. I'd be doing the tap dance routine I learned in the fourth grade."

By now, he was standing in the kitchen, an expanse of granite countertops and white cabinets, expensive built-in appliances. There was a row of stools in front of an island so I took one and he took another at the far end, with a space between us.

"Like I told your..."

"Sister."

"Your sister," he said. "I don't know what happened to Dave. I worked all day yesterday, went out with friends for dinner and drinks. They can vouch for me."

I had figured as much. He wouldn't have let me in if he hadn't had an ironclad alibi.

"Tell me about the trouble between you and Dave," I said, cutting to the chase.

A little vein popped out on his forehead and I wondered if he used steroids to pump up his muscles. Or some of those medications that made the veins on your arms swell up. Because you know how much the ladies love those.

He looked at the ceiling, and I wondered if he was examining the vast array of built-in lighting or the elaborate crown molding.

"You want to know the best thing I ever did to become a successful doctor?" he asked.

"Medical school?"

He shook his head. "My undergrad I double majored in pre-med and business. I took a lot of business courses because I knew that's what separated the good and bad medical practices. I worked briefly at one that was so chaotic I couldn't believe it. Horrible organization, systems inefficiencies and a joke of accounting practices."

"It's a business," I said. "Being a doctor."

"Damn right it is. So Dave and I were always on the same page about that stuff. Our practice, along with the seven other doctors, was a well-oiled machine, thanks in no small part to my training. There are plenty of good doctors, but not all of them are great business owners. You have to be both."

"Was Dave good at both?"

"Absolutely, until about six months ago," he said.

I sensed genuine sadness on his part.

"What happened?"

"One day he came in to me with a new, highly aggressive plan to expand the practice. Multiple new offices, new docs, etc. He said that he'd been thinking about this for a long time and thought it was a fantastic plan."

"I take it you didn't agree."

"Not at all," Kemp said. "It was a fucking horrible plan. He hadn't done his research, his market analysis, cost projections. It looked like something he'd thrown together on a meth binge."

I winced a little at the reference. I was still raw from losing Dave, but I could see the anger in Kemp's face.

"Not only that," he continued. "It went against everything we had always agreed on. Our patients were happy and frankly, we had more business than we could handle. You have to weigh customer satisfaction, workload and profitability. All of the partners were making excellent money. Not internet-billionaire money, but plenty."

It seemed out of character for Dave. Although he was fun-loving, I also knew he was fairly conservative with his money.

"What did you tell him?" I asked.

"I told him he was out of his mind. I had no desire to expand and even if I did, his plan was a piece of shit. It would take at least a year or two of intense planning to grow the practice even more, which I had no desire to do. It would require even more money spent on lawyers, not to mention accountants and real estate agents. And I knew the other docs felt the same way."

Kemp slid off his kitchen stool and began pacing. He looked like he was warming up to do a major squat press or deadlift.

"How did he take it?"

"Badly. At first, he seemed to understand, but then he repeatedly came back at me over the next couple of weeks, each time more aggressive than the time before but I stuck to my guns."

"Did he say why he suddenly wanted to expand the practice?"

Kemp nodded. "It was in a moment of weakness, I think. He'd been really hard on me, arguing, getting snarky. And then one day, his face kind of became really sad and depressed. And he looked at me. He said he was going to be totally straight with me. And then his voice got really soft and he told me he really needed the money."

"He needed the money?" I found that hard to believe. Dave was super successful. I knew he had a shitload of cash.

"That's what he said. He needed the money. I offered him a loan and then he got really pissed and threatened me."

"*He* threatened *you?*"

Christine had told me just the opposite.

"First professionally, as in he was going to boot me out of the practice if I didn't go along with the plan, something he would never be able to do. We are, were, way too linked. It would have taken a team of lawyers months to separate us."

"And then?"

"Then he threatened me personally. Said he was going to kick my ass."

I leaned back. That really didn't sound like Dave. Dave had been an athlete, a tight end in football at a small college in Ohio, but he was not the kind to pick a physical fight."

"What did you say?"

Kemp smiled at me, and this time I saw something different in his eyes. Not quite predatory, but a vibe that communicated ruthlessness.

"I told him two words: any time."

CHAPTER THIRTEEN

Angelo Flores was no stranger to blackouts. He'd had some doozies that when he'd first gone to a treatment group and told the stories, the other junkies had howled. Probably the best one was when he came out of a drunk and he was standing in front of a jury, making his closing statement and he had no idea who his client was or what he'd done. The jury had looked at him, and then he'd looked at his client and then the judge and said, "The defense rests."

He hadn't rested, though. He never had. By then he was on the prowl night and day for the next high.

So he was no stranger to blackouts. He'd lived through all of them, and what a bizarre litany they were.

But this one, this one was strange.

His eyes slowly creaked open like a garage door in the middle of a frigid winter. Creaking and groaning, his eyes and mind winced at the bright sunlight.

Not sunlight.

Electric lights.

Several of them, bright and intense, pointing at him.

His first thought was that he'd been arrested (again) and was now being interrogated by the police.

But somehow, that didn't seem right.

Angelo tried to swallow but his mouth was dry and his tongue was swollen. His head ached with an intense pain he instantly recognized as very different from what he was used to. What had that friend of his shot him up with? Angelo had assumed it was heroin, maybe it wasn't.

Now, he looked around. But he couldn't see anything. The lights were so bright and there was a noise that penetrated his ears. He tried shouting but couldn't hear himself.

For the first time in a long time, Angelo Flores was scared.

It was apparently a moment of firsts because he suddenly thought of his wife. Or ex-wife, actually. Nicole was a fair-haired beauty, with pale skin and auburn hair. Beautiful green eyes. They'd always made an interesting couple, he, Angelo, dark to the point of being almost swarthy. While she, Nicole, was the epitome of a beautiful Irish lass. They'd met at a holiday party the law firm had thrown for all of its clients. At the time, she was an assistant to the president of one of the firm's biggest clients and Angelo was a young, hungry attorney. They'd seen something in each other and a year later they were married.

It saddened him to think of her and how they'd been at the beginning. How naïve they both had been. Who could have predicted that the marriage would collapse and Angelo would wind up a junkie?

The sadness vanished as his hardened heart exerted its ability to deflect pain. The other pain was real. A deep, throbbing pain in his body, extending out to his limbs.

How could his entire body hurt?

Angelo tried to look down at the rest of his body, but he couldn't see. Something was covering his face, but it didn't really matter because he knew what was happening. Not just by the pain, but from the smell.

He was being burned alive.

CHAPTER FOURTEEN

The restaurant went by the name of the Casa Maya Grill and it was well known for serving authentic Mexican food with a nod to the Yucatan Peninsula.

Nate Becker, my friend of many years and owner of several news-related websites, was a big fan. I had agreed to buy him lunch there, against the best wishes of my budget. In fact, whenever I scheduled a meal with Nate Becker, the Rockne food bill pretty much doubled.

Nate was more than just a lover of food, he was an obsessive stalker of food. He woke up thinking about what he would have for breakfast, and then halfway through breakfast, would start thinking about lunch with the pattern repeating itself for the rest of the day.

He didn't have a day planner, he had a meal planner.

Even before his child had some health issues that created a lot of stress for Nate, he'd always been into food. A big eater. He had been born and raised in Michigan and in the Midwest, being able to pack away food was often seen as a positive character trait. I'd been to Los Angeles a couple of times and there, it's the complete opposite. In LA, they race to be the first one to push away a plate full of half-eaten food and claim to be "stuffed."

Like always, Nate had arrived before me. He was my height, but about twice as broad. If Nate was a boat, you would say he had an impressive beam and would be solid in the water. Today he had on jeans, a flannel shirt and his salt-and-pepper hair was long and a bit wild. He had a thick beard, as well. All-in-all, he looked like an unemployed lumberjack rather than a highly perceptive journalist and very talented writer.

He had picked a table in the back and he sat with his back to the wall, so he could see who was arriving. His notepad and pen were never far from his reach.

I slid in across from him.

"Is food from the Yucatan really that different from regular Mexican food?" I asked as I settled in.

"Of course it, John," he replied with a sigh. "Otherwise they wouldn't bother mentioning it."

"What if it's just a marketing ploy?"

Nate had been trying unsuccessfully for years to try to turn me into a foodie but it just wasn't happening. I was a plain old meat-and-potatoes kind of guy who'd been eating salads more often of late due to comments from my better half.

"Like what?"

"I don't even want to try to talk about Mayan influences, the Spanish, and instances of Dutch flavorings in food from the Yucatan. It would be lost on you. Suffice to say, they smoke a lot more food and obviously a lot of great seafood dishes."

He could have fooled me. There were chips, salsa and guacamole, and as good as they were, tasted just like every other kind of chips, salsa and guacamole I'd ever had.

"So what are you working on these days?" I asked him.

Nate was a great source for me, and really a lot more than that. His vast knowledge of not only Grosse Pointe but Detroit as well, had come in handy on many, many cases. These meals, which I always paid for, was my way of thanking him for his help.

"Oh, the usual corruption downtown," he said. It seemed like there were always new stories about kickbacks and bribes in the government of Detroit. "But there's a rumor someone is killing hookers again," he said.

A few years back, there had been a serial killer loose in Detroit and his prey of choice had been the many hookers who plied their trade in the Motor City. He'd been caught, eventually, and his tally had been somewhere around ten prostitutes murdered.

"New cases? New victims?" I asked, meaning they weren't just newly discovered remains from the old case.

Nate nodded.

"That's the rumor, but I don't have any facts, yet." A waiter delivered our food and just before Nate tucked into his enchiladas, he asked, "What about you? The Dave Ingells case?"

I nodded. Even though Nate hadn't really known Dave, he'd met him a time or two. "Yeah, I don't have a client but I'm helping out however I can," I said. "Don't want to get in Ellen's way, though."

"No one wants to get in Ellen's way," Nate said. He knew Ellen pretty well, what with being a reporter, but he'd also been around her at my house a few times. "I've got feelers out on Dave's case, too," he added. "I'll let you know if I hear anything. So far, nada."

We both ate in silence for a few minutes.

"What did I order again?" I asked.

"Pibil," Nate said. "It's a staple of the Yucatan diet."

"It's delicious."

It was a burrito filled with pork that had been smothered in some sort of spicy, smoky red sauce.

"The Ingells case is interesting, you know," Nate said. "Unlike the hookers, which you know is almost totally random, there's no way Dave's murder was. Of course, there are always exceptions, but the guy was fairly squeaky clean, right?"

I hesitated for the briefest moment, thinking about what Anna had said, but I decided to keep that to myself for now.

"Yeah, Mr. Clean."

"The idea that someone would abduct a healthy adult male in Grosse Pointe, drive him to Detroit, strangle him and dump the body, are pretty slim," Nate opined. "I say Dave knew his killer, for sure."

Unlike cops and detectives, whose guiding principle was to avoid jumping to early conclusions, Nate was a reporter. He could speculate all he wanted.

But I had to agree with him.

Dave probably knew his killer.

The question was, did I?

CHAPTER FIFTEEN

Christine Ingells had no desire to be questioned yet again by me, certainly not in her house and certainly not in front of her children. So she agreed to meet me at Patterson Park, one of two city parks in Grosse Pointe set along Lake St. Clair.

The lake and I had a tortured history. It's where the body of Benjamin Collins had been found, after I'd unwittingly returned him to his killer. His life had ended, and mine was changed forever.

Now, I got to the park early, walked past the little splash pad where it was too cold for any little kids to play, and the giant wood play structure. There was a breeze coming off the lake, crisp and sharp, hinting of much colder weather on the way.

Walking past the permanent charcoal grills, most of them rusty and sad, and the now-empty kayak racks near the gate to the kayak launch, I stepped up onto the boardwalk that ran along the lake's edge. The water was dark and choppy, white foam curling over the dark crests of the waves' bodies.

The boardwalk was empty and I took a seat at the first

bench, a section widened out from the boardwalk and projected over the rocky bank of the lake. Tall grass had grown up, partially obscuring the water.

A giant freighter nosed its way out from the Detroit side of the lake, heading north. The channel had been dredged through the otherwise shallow lake, nearly thirty-five feet in depth. The rest of the lake averaged between seven and fifteen feet deep. But it was still a big body of water, some thirty miles across in parts.

I heard footsteps on the boardwalk, turned, and saw Christine Ingells walking toward me. She had on blue jeans and a dark black sweater with pockets into which she had thrust her hands. Her shoulders were hunched against the cold. Her pale face stuck out in the fading light.

We embraced and then each took a seat on the bench. I could smell her perfume and it was a lovely scent, set against the natural backdrop of the lake.

"How are you holding up?" I asked.

She shrugged her shoulders. "As well as can be expected, I guess," she replied, her voice soft and a little bit hoarse. "The girls are in a state of shock. Everyone's home now and we go from laughing hysterically one moment to crying our eyes out the next. I guess that's how grief works."

Words of comfort were needed, but they just didn't find their way out of my mouth. It just seemed like anything I could say would be lame.

"What did you want to talk about?" she said.

"What you're going through is horrible," I said. "I'm going through it too, on a much different level. Dave and I were just friends."

"A lot of people are going to miss him," she said. "That's one of the things I loved about him. He was good with people because I think they sensed his innate goodness."

"You're right," I said. "He was one of those guys you knew you could trust when the chips were down."

She sighed but it was shaky, a precursor to crying.

"You didn't invite me out here to talk about what a great guy Dave was, though, did you?"

"No, I'm afraid I didn't even though I could talk for hours about him," I answered. "I talked to Barry Kemp and he told me some things that I figured aren't true but I'd like you to confirm that for me."

"What did he say?" she asked. Her voice had taken on an edge and I knew I had to be careful here. Grief could turn to rage in an instant and I didn't want to be responsible for causing Christine even more emotional trauma.

"For starters, he insinuated that Dave wanted to expand the practice."

She tilted her head to the side as she thought about it. "Not really. I mean, he talked about it occasionally, but he was pretty happy with the state of the business. And, I mean, you knew Dave. Being there to see all of the girls' games was pretty important. He often said that opening up any more offices would probably result in him being gone for that kind of stuff. So yeah, he had mentioned it in theory, but then he usually shot down the idea because family was more important to him than more money."

I knew Dave rarely missed family events. Especially when it came to his kids' sports.

"So you guys were okay financially?" I asked.

She laughed and looked at me. "Yeah, of course. What, did Barry say we weren't?"

Now it was my turn to look out at the lake. "Not in those words," I said. "But he kind of hinted that Dave was really eager to expand and increase revenues."

"Barry's full of shit," she said. "It was just the opposite. Dave told me that was the reason for the fallout between them. Barry wanted to expand, Dave didn't. Barry needed the money. For what, who knows?"

If Barry Kemp had lied to me, it certainly wouldn't surprise me. In fact, he had used the truth about himself to project a falsehood onto Dave. That, too was an old trick.

I sensed there was more to the story than what she was telling me. "Did Dave have any theories about why Barry needed cash?"

"None that he actually came out with, but there were always rumors Barry had a pretty extravagant lifestyle," Christine said. "Probably because he was so private. I have no idea if they were true or not."

A part of me wondered if Barry had sent me on a wild goose chase, or if he really believed what he told me. It was amazing how often human beings project their own failings onto others and be completely oblivious to it. I had seen it dozens of times.

A phone buzzed and Christine reached into the pocket of her sweater. The light from it illuminated her face and I saw how tired she looked as she read the screen.

"I have to go," she said and got to her feet. "Do you need to ask me anything else?"

"No, I'll walk you back," I said and we made our way through the dark park. We didn't say anything else.

The only sound was the lake and its waves hurling themselves onto the rocks.

CHAPTER SIXTEEN

At times, my relationship with my sister seemed illicit. Oh, it was fine for her to come to my house and vice versa, but we tended to avoid being seen in public together.

The Starbucks in the village, for instance, was far too busy with locals. Everyone knew we were brother and sister, but professionally, for Ellen, it could be taken the wrong way.

So, she invited me to her house for coffee.

Ellen's house was a cool Craftsman bungalow with a wide porch and tons of natural woodwork. She'd remodeled it herself and it was a beauty.

The back door was unlocked and I gave a quick knock then went inside. Ellen was at the coffee pot, pouring both of us a cup.

"I wish you hadn't knocked," she said. "That way I could have shot you."

"You probably would have missed," I answered. "I've been working out and I'm practically a twig."

She pushed a mug across the counter toward me.

"Here, have a cup," she said. "You could always add some

protein powder. I know how you bodybuilders love that crap."

I picked up the cup and followed her into the living room where a pair of Stickley rockers sat kitty corner, with a leather couch between them. We each took a rocker.

"Whatever happened to Jeff?" I asked her. Jeff had been her last boyfriend, he'd lasted about six months. Men tended to be intimidated by Ellen. I couldn't blame them. She was downright mean most of the time. I couldn't help it if I'd gotten all of the Rockne charm, her portion included.

"He referred to me as 'arm candy' and while on the one hand I was flattered, I also told him that an arm usually has a fist, and maybe he'd like a candy fist you know where."

I winced.

"Needless to say, that was all she wrote for Jeff."

"I wish Anna would refer to me as arm candy. Who doesn't love candy?"

We sat in silence for a minute.

"I talked to Christine Ingells last night," I offered.

"And?"

"She pretty much contradicted everything Barry Kemp told me. Dave didn't want to expand the practice, Barry did. Dave wasn't in any kind of financial trouble, Barry needed money. There were rumors about Barry's lifestyle demanding lots of cash."

"Wouldn't surprise me at all," Ellen said. "I got that kind of vibe from Kemp. We ran him through the database and while there was nothing major, there were a few drunk and disorderlies from a decade ago."

"Maybe he grew up."

"Nah, he's a man child if I ever saw one. Speaking of body-builders, you think he works out all the time for his health? Hell, no. He wants women, or maybe men, to look at his body like it's a sexual playground."

"Great name for a band," I offered. "And now, live from the Fillmore, Sexual Playground!"

I started banging my head in rhythm to a song.

"Speaking of man children," Ellen said.

"I know you didn't invite me over here to insult me," I said. "Wait, you probably did."

"No, that's just a little icing on the side," she said. "Actually, I want you to do me a favor."

"I don't believe in favoritism."

She got up and walked past me, then returned with a couple sheets of paper that she dropped into my lap.

"Take a look at the different places Dave's cell phone bounced. It was all over Detroit and we don't have the manpower to send people out checking these locations. Most of them are bars and restaurants from an initial look. But maybe there's a link we're missing. I figured you've got plenty of time on your hands."

"I didn't know there was room in the Grosse Pointe Police Department budget to hire a PI."

She ignored me as we both knew I wouldn't be paid for this.

"Anything else?" I asked.

"Yeah, try not to get shot in Detroit. Anna would be pissed at me."

CHAPTER SEVENTEEN

Could you trust a guy like Barry Kemp? A doctor with a passion for bodybuilding and who had a falling out with a partner over whether or not to expand the practice?

It was easy for me not to trust him.

I knew Dave and Dave was a standup guy. If someone had a problem with him, that said more about them than Dave.

Still, I knew I was biased.

As I drove away from Ellen's house, I thought about my next step.

The truth was, something was nagging me about Barry Kemp. No, not the overcompensating, steroid-abusing aspect of his personality. Something else. I thought back to the parties at Dave's house where I'd met him. Had Dave mentioned something about him to me?

No, that wasn't it.

It was really going to bug me.

To take my mind off it for the moment, I pulled out the sheet Ellen had given me that showed the different locations Dave's cell phone had been. I say his cell phone, because who knew if it was in Dave's possession at the time? Maybe Dave was already dead by the time his phone was dragged all over the city.

Even so, if that was the case, it would at least maybe tell me what the killer was doing, if I could put together some kind of logic between the paths the phone had taken.

I drove to Jefferson Avenue, turned right, and headed toward downtown Detroit. Once I crossed the border at Alter from Grosse Pointe into the city things changed rapidly. The buildings along Jefferson were mostly abandoned, with neighborhoods branching off on either side. Most of the homes directly bordering Jefferson were abandoned as well.

The businesses doing well were the liquor stores and convenience stores, as well as fast food.

A developer had purchased large tracts of land near Grosse Pointe and development had begun in places. A few large tracts of land had been cleared of chest-high grass and weeds, replaced with flat expanses of dirt, and a few piles of preconstruction materials.

I wondered how long it would take the redevelopment to reach Jefferson Avenue.

The first address where Dave's phone had pinged was near a street called St. Aubin. I got there, then turned left and made my way down toward the river. This was a mixed-use area with some new restaurants and a brewpub going in recently. However, there were still a lot of empty, uninhabited warehouses.

What the hell was Dave doing down here? I could see him going to a brewpub, the guy liked beer as much as the rest of us. But to be down here on a Thursday night, close to midnight? Didn't make a lot of sense to me. Plus, he obviously hadn't told Christine or she would have mentioned it.

Finally, my GPS brought me to the exact point where Dave's phone had been.

Weird.

It was an intersection with vacant lots on three of the four corners. To my left, was a warehouse of some sort painted black, with blackened windows. There were chains on the doors and the windows sported security bars. There was garbage scattered about and it looked like there hadn't been a human being around in the last decade or so.

I pulled half up onto the crumbling remains of a sidewalk – who would walk around down here – and got out, locking the car behind me.

Not the best place to be, even now, in the morning. I wondered when angry, homeless junkies were more dangerous – at night? Or in the morning when they might wake up with their addiction clamoring for relief?

There was no point in wandering around the vacant lots, it was the empty warehouse that caught my eye. If Dave had been here for any reason, this would have been the only thing he could have gone into. Unless he wanted to go sprawl out in the empty lots and take a nap.

I walked up to the twin doors and tested the chain with its lock. Sturdy, and still locked. No sign of recent entry. In fact, the cement from what was maybe a driveway at one point was now buckled, and a huge chunk of it protruded upwards, effectively blocking the doors from getting open.

So no one had opened these doors recently.

And, by recently, I meant years.

A quick peek around the edge of the warehouse's exterior showed it ran the length of the block. I tried the other way, and it was the same, except halfway down I could see there was maybe a courtyard of some sort. I followed it along until the space opened up and I saw a rusty picnic table with its top removed, empty beer cans and a broken floor-to-ceiling window.

An entrance.

Now I got a little nervous. It was one thing to walk around outside, but to go in? It didn't seem like a good idea.

Well, I never really listened to that little voice that warned me about doing stupid things. Because if I did, I never would have asked out Pam Hitchins while she was dating Jack Wang. Jack Wang knew tae kwon do and he kicked the shit out of me.

On that note, I ducked through the window into darkness.

What was I worried about?

It was fine.

The place had been stripped clean and it was totally empty. I walked the length of the space from one end to the other and all I found was a used condom and more empty beer cans. Apparently someone threw their litter everywhere, but were very careful with their seed. Strange contradiction.

Had Dave been here? And if so, why?

Something seemed off about the place, but I couldn't figure out what it was. I heard a movement behind me and turned.

A rat the size of an armadillo ran across the concrete floor.

Rats were the worst. I've never forgiven them for the Black Plague.

Outside, I walked back to my car and was relieved to see no one had smashed my windows to get inside and find nothing but an empty pack of gum.

Behind the wheel, I thought about what to do. The next address on the list was, at first glance, right next to Ford Field where the Detroit Lions liked to lose football games.

Knowing full well Dave hadn't attended a night game as there wasn't one that night, I put the car in gear nonetheless.

I glanced over at the river as I drove parallel to Jefferson, waiting for a cross street. My mind wandered to Barry Kemp and suddenly, I realized what it was he'd said that had been nagging at me.

It was when he was trying to convince me that Dave had accosted him with this aggressive plan to expand the practice. He'd said something about how it would require him to spend 'more' money on lawyers.

I knew Dave pretty well, and if he had been in some sort of legal trouble, he would have told me. So when Barry had talked about spending even more on lawyers, something in the back of my mind wondered what he meant. I think I knew now. He was talking about himself. About how he was already spending money on lawyers.

It begged the question: why?

Ellen had mentioned Barry having some trouble way in the past, as in over ten years ago.

Was it something with his medical practice?

Or was it personal?

Ellen's official police check on Barry Kemp would have only revealed active problems. Maybe there was something else going on with Barry Kemp. Something that required lots of attorneys.

I picked up the phone.

It was time to do my own squat press on the little guy.

CHAPTER EIGHTEEN

My car had a Bluetooth connection so when I was put on hold trying to talk to Barry Kemp, I was able to maneuver the sometimes challenging job of driving to Ford Field.

It's not that Detroit drivers are bad, it's that a lot of them just don't care.

There are a lot of folks in what is often referred to as the capital of the rust belt who are going through very hard times. Hence, they have some really shitty cars. And if you drive a shitty car, you don't really care much if you collide with someone who's driving a nicer vehicle. Part of the reason why is that you also can't afford insurance and a lawsuit will net your persecutor absolutely nothing.

Therefore, you don't have to follow any traffic rules at all.

Don't use a signal.

Change lanes without looking.

Blow through red lights.

Talk on a cell phone that's worth more than the car you're driving.

Put on horrible makeup and/or adjust your wig while driving.

Or my personal favorite, chug from a pint of Night Train while you're behind the wheel.

Eventually, I caught sight of the newish Ford Field stadium exterior and found a parking space nearby. It was mid-morning and the place was nearly as deserted as the warehouse I'd just visited. I saw a beggar a block ahead shuffle across the street and a smartly dressed couple walking briskly somewhere.

"Mr. Rockne?" the voice boomed from my car's speakers and I jumped. They hadn't used hold music and I had let my mind wander. Barry Kemp's receptionist or secretary or assistant, whatever you wanted to call her, had a voice that cut through the clutter.

"Yeah?"

Up ahead the beggar turned as the couple crossed the street. He said something to them but they kept going without looking at him.

"Dr. Kemp is unavailable, I'm afraid."

"It took you twenty minutes to figure that out?" I was exaggerating a little, it was only about seven minutes or so, but it had felt like a long time. Way too long for the answer she provided.

"Yes, I apologize for the wait, but Dr. Kemp was with a patient."

"So he finished with the patient and then told you to tell me that he's unavailable?"

When she spoke again, it was with an obviously perturbed tone. "May I take a message, Mr. Rockne?"

"Tell him to call me. I have information on one of his very important pending legal matters."

It was total bullshit, but I had a hunch.

"I'll pass along the message," she said, followed with a very enthusiastic click.

I turned off my phone's Bluetooth to conserve the battery

and got out of the car. I jogged up to where the homeless guy was now sitting on the sidewalk, his back against the wall of a bar that was closed.

"Spare change?" he asked as I approached.

From my wallet, I withdrew a twenty-dollar bill. I held it in my hand while with my other hand I scrolled the photos on my phone until I came across a good one of Dave. I blew it up and turned the phone to face the beggar.

Getting a good look at him I saw that he was younger than I thought, although from his apparent lifestyle I'm sure his years had aged him even more. Still, he couldn't have been beyond his thirties. Maybe early forties at the most.

He had on black pants, a hooded sweatshirt and dirty Timberland boots without shoelaces. I saw newspaper sticking out from the leg of his pants.

"Have you seen this guy around at all? Maybe Thursday night?"

The guy squinted. The wind shifted and I got a really good whiff of him, making me wish I had a portable bottle of Febreze.

"Shit, I don't know, man."

What the hell. I handed him the twenty and one of my business cards, although I doubted he had a cell phone in his pocket.

"Haven't seen him?" I asked again. "Were you down here Thursday night?"

"Shit, I'm down here every night, morning and day, brother," he said.

"Was anything unusual going on?"

"You kiddin' me? Weird shit goes down here all the time!" he cackled a little bit. "People disappear like smoke down here. One minute you crackin' wise with a fool, next minute you standing there with your dick in your hand like some crazy bitch done stole your mind!"

"Excellent observations," I said.

"Best part?" he continued. "White people the craziest of 'em all. You muthafucks, what they say, unpredictable as shit? Runnin' around drunk, high, half-naked pukin' in the gutters, wrecking cars. Oughta be a law against white people. Stay outta the city. We afraid of y'all."

A stream of urine began to leak out of his pants, and I saw the newspaper catching some of it before it fell onto the sidewalk. It was an editorial and I wondered if the homeless guy was providing his opinion on the article.

"Well, if you think of something and can find a phone, call the number on that card I gave you," I said.

Back at the car, I looked over my shoulder.

The homeless guy was gone.

He'd disappeared like smoke.

CHAPTER NINETEEN

It took me a few more hours to hit all of the stops on the Dave Ingells cell phone tour, but they were all abandoned lots.

You'd be surprised how many of them there are in Detroit. There are entire city blocks now home to mostly weeds and rubble.

Occasionally, you'll find a developer brave enough to start putting up some new homes, which then look like movie sets, temporarily placed on a barren studio lot.

I did check them all out, though.

Mostly what I did was scare some rats and even send some pheasant running for more cover. The city of Detroit, with its thousands upon thousands of abandoned city blocks and long grass, was home to a surprising amount of wildlife, not just the human kind.

Hell, there were coyotes in Grosse Pointe. Often times spotted on the Detroit Country Club fairways. I always wondered if they were dressed in goofy golf outfits.

Ellen wasn't answering her phone, or should I saw she

wasn't answering my calls, so I left a message stating what I'd found, which was basically a big heaping bag o' nothing.

Retracing my route I went back down to Jefferson and followed that all the way into Grosse Pointe, hooking a left on Cadieux to my office. I parked, climbed the stairs and went inside.

Too early for a beer so I grabbed a Diet Coke and launched the web browser on my computer.

Using the usual method of searching the hell out of Google results, I basically came up empty on Dr. Barry Kemp. Oh, there were the usual anonymous doctor recommendations and reviews, most of them positive. Kemp had at various times donated money to certain charities, which was well-publicized.

It was all smoke and mirrors.

I wanted to find out the truth regarding the real Dr. Barry Kemp.

Starting with his name.

Was Barry really his full name? Or was it short for something? Barack Obama had been called Barry when he was young.

Maybe Barry Kemp had been called something different.

I tried Brent Kemp, Bart Kemp and in the process, I discovered a link mentioning Bertram Kemp.

It caught my eye.

Not because it was a strange name, but mainly because it was in reference to a bodybuilding competition.

The link provided almost no information, so this time I Googled 'Bertram Kemp' and quite a few more entries populated my screen. There were the drunk and disorderlies my sister, Ellen, had mentioned, as well as bodybuilding forum mentions and a few links to dating/hookup websites.

Barry was Bertram.

Did Ellen already know this? If so, why hadn't she shared that information with me? I would follow up with her later.

In the meantime, I figured that while Barry Kemp might not agree to meet with me, I had a feeling Bertram would be more receptive.

Probably my greatest attribute that qualified me for being a good private investigator was the fact that I simply loved annoying the hell out of people. It brought me great mirth and personal satisfaction.

So I gleefully called back Kemp's office and even got the same stubborn phone lady to talk to me.

This time I said the magic words.

"Could I speak to Bertram Kemp, please?" I asked, adding a little huskiness to my voice by channeling Kathleen Turner in Body Heat.

It was no surprise that it took awhile, I figured she had to wait to talk to him, and then mention that the caller had specifically requested a chat with Bertram.

Would he take the call?

Was she on standing orders to put through anyone who referred to him as Bertram?

The hell if I knew.

But half of the successes I've had ended up coming from me just winging it.

"This is Dr. Kemp," Barry said to me on the phone.

"Hi Barry, it's John Rockne," I said. There was no point in asking for permission to plow ahead. "You mentioned to me that you didn't want to spend more money on lawyers. What did you mean by that? Are you currently involved with any pending lawsuits?"

"This is ridiculous," he said. "I'm trying to run a business here."

"I am, too," I said. "Trying to run a business that is. It's extremely difficult in these trying financial times–"

I heard a door close in the background and figured Barry had closed himself in his office for more privacy.

"Why are you so concerned with me? Didn't you check out where I was when Dave disappeared?" he asked, his voice chock full of annoyance verging on anger. "I was with friends all night. Surely the police know that. Why don't you?"

Kemp was talking to me with the clear knowledge that I was probably sharing information with Ellen, who just happened to be the lead investigator on the case. He was trying to influence her through me. Good luck with that.

"I have every reason to believe you had nothing to do with Dave's death," I lied. "I'm just tying up some loose ends, that's all. So, back to my original question. Are you involved with any pending legal issues?"

He sighed. "I don't have to answer that."

"You don't have to," I said. "But you can."

"No," he said. "No pending legal matter. I certainly have an attorney on retainer, but there are no pending cases."

"Who is your attorney?"

A pause. "The firm is called Gadlicke & Associates."

"Gadlicke?"

"Yes."

"What a weird name."

"I've really got to get back to work," he said.

"Anything else you want to tell me?" I asked.

"Not at all," he said and hung up on me.

I was pissed. I wanted to refer to him as Bertram.

CHAPTER TWENTY

Look, if you're born and given the name Bertram, you're going to cause trouble. If not, you're going to get beaten up quite often. It made perfect sense to me that Barry Kemp didn't use his real name and it also didn't shock me that he'd become a bodybuilder.

He'd had no choice, after all, once his parents had dubbed him Bertram.

I guess he could've gone by Burt. Or Bertie. Dr. Bertie. It sounded like a cartoon character. "And now kids, we're going to pay a visit to Dr. Bertie!"

His attorney wasn't much better. Gadlicke.

Sounded like a drunken fraternity game.

Now back in my office, a quick search of Google didn't tell me much. Gadlicke & Associates was a firm out in Bloomfield Hills. Fairly large, I saw photos of about fifteen lawyers or so and it looked like they covered just about every kind of law one might need. Corporate. Tax. Personal Liability. Real Estate.

Nothing outrageous showed up in the search results,

either. No celebrity cases, murder trials, famous political scandals where Gadlicke & Associates were involved.

It was interesting to me that medical malpractice was included in the firm's laundry list of services provided. Had Dr. Kemp botched some sort of surgery?

Trying to talk to an attorney about one of their clients clearly wasn't an option.

Federal lawsuits were easy to search thanks to PACER, an online database of court cases. Local jurisdictions were all on their own, however, and I didn't have time to plow through individual town, city, and county databases. I did, however, have another option.

A former client of mine had been accused of stealing proprietary computer software from her employer, which wasn't the case at all. My client had actually been planning to start her own business and her employer was afraid of the competition. I'd gotten proof that the owner had falsely accused my client, and the charges were dropped.

My client, the daughter of a refugee from Vietnam, was a young woman by the name of Chia Pham. She had been very happy to have her legal issue resolved and her business was now doing well.

She was a bit of a computer genius and had offered me her services if I ever needed her help. So I shot her a quick email asking her to see if she could find any evidence of a Dr. Barry (or Bertram) Kemp involved in any current lawsuits, or lawsuits that had been closed within the past five years.

In a p.s., I added that she should quote me a price as I meant to hire her for the information.

With that, I decided that the too-early-for-a-beer window had closed, so I reached into the little fridge by my desk and pulled out a Point beer. I twisted off the top and took a long drink.

I made an imaginary toast to Dave and tried not to think about where he was right then.

Right now, I had only questions and no answers. It was progress that I at least had someone who had a grudge against Dave. But I also had a hard time imagining Barry Kemp strangling Dave with a rope. It just didn't seem like he was the kind of guy who liked to get his hands dirty. Plus, he had an alibi.

So why was Dave's cell phone pinging all around Detroit the night of his death? What was that all about?

Another long drink of Point beer didn't provide any answers.

My cell phone rang and I wondered if it might be Chi Chi, which was my girl Chi Pham's nickname.

It wasn't.

It was a number I didn't recognize.

"Rockne?"

It took me a minute to place the voice.

"Barry?" I asked.

"Look, I need to talk to you."

"Isn't that what we're doing?"

"Don't be a smart-ass. In person. It's important." Barry Kemp sounded strangely distraught.

"How important?" I asked. "Like drive-to-Royal-Oak important?"

I could hear some vague traffic noise in the background and I assumed he was driving. Someone honking their horn confirmed my suspicion.

"Yeah, I want to hire you," he said. "But I need to see you as soon as possible, first."

I pulled the phone away from my ear and looked at the screen, then replaced it.

"What?"

"Meet me at my house. I have an idea of what might have

happened, but I can't tell you over the phone. We need to meet, and then I want to hire you to prove my theory."

"You can't just give me a synopsis of your theory?"

He cursed under his breath and I thought he was saying it to me, but then I realized he was fighting traffic.

"Do you always fight with potential clients?" he asked. "Is that good for your business?

No, I wanted to say. *Just the ones who are under suspicion of murder.*

"Okay, where do you want to meet?" I asked.

"My house, that's where I'm going now. I'll be home in ten minutes."

I took a quick look at the clock. Not quite rush hour yet. "Okay, I'll try to be there in a half hour or so."

We disconnected and I finished off my beer.

This time, I was going to call him Bertram to his face.

CHAPTER TWENTY-ONE

With the office locked, I went down the stairs and out to my car, fired it up and turned onto Cadieux. From there, I hit the freeway. As I drove, I thought about Kemp's strange offer.

He wanted to hire me.

It reminded me how after O.J. Simpson was found innocent, he vowed that he would spend the rest of his life trying to bring the real killers to justice. No one really believed that, especially how the only images of him from then on showed him on a golf course. Maybe he thought the real killers were golfers.

It was an age-old tactic. If you're accused of something, and especially if you're guilty of something, claim you're working hard to find the true guilty parties.

It was usually a smokescreen and nothing else.

However, Barry could have accomplished that without wanting to meet me. He could have done it over the phone. Which made me at least consider that he wasn't putting on a public relations show, after all he had to know that I would try to poke holes in whatever fake story he was promoting in order to help me take the suspicion off him.

I exited the freeway, turned onto Royal Oak's main street, and eventually got to Barry Kemp's house. I parked on the curb and studied the neighborhood. Nothing had changed, except that day had been bright and sunny and now a light rain had begun to fall, with dark clouds overhead. It was funny how different a place could feel depending on what the weather was like. Barry's neighborhood didn't seem quite so cool and sophisticated. Now it looked a little old and tired.

This was going to be interesting, I thought, as I got out of the car, locked it and walked up to Kemp's front door. I rang the bell and waited. Slipping my phone from my pocket, I confirmed that he hadn't texted a cancellation.

I knocked on the door, my knuckles producing a fair amount of volume for the effort.

Again, no answer.

I reached down and tested the door. It was unlocked. I opened it a crack.

"Barry?"

No answer.

"Bertram?"

Still no answer.

Probably in the weight room, pumping iron. I had no idea if there was a weight room, but it seemed like a good guess. However, I didn't hear any telltale sounds of metal clanking and grunting and groaning.

The phone was still in my hand and I considered calling 911 or Ellen. What would I say, though? Someone left a door open? Ellen would give me shit about being here in the first place.

I thought about my gun, locked in the gun safe back in my office. I really needed to get into the habit of carrying it.

Oh, well. I stepped into Barry Kemp's house and closed the door behind me. I heard nothing and it smelled clean, like it had just been visited by a team of anal-retentive maids.

It was sparse, but that was by design. I was struck again by the modern furniture, the absence of any clutter. No kids. No dogs. No cats. Just a neat freak who probably ate out every night and spent most of his free time at the gym, unless he had a home gym, which I suspected might be the case.

The house was set up with a foyer that opened up onto a living room on the left, a kitchen straight ahead and another hallway that branched off to the right. I assumed the bedrooms were to the right, or maybe a powder room.

"Barry?" I called out again.

I followed the hallway into the kitchen, spotting the five thousand dollar espresso maker and pristine countertops. No sign of life, or cooking.

Something made me hesitate. The living room and kitchen were very public places, to go any deeper into the house was truly a violation of privacy and something I wasn't all that comfortable with. Not to mention it was technically a violation of the law and if someone was really angry with me, could cost me my PI license.

I did it anyway.

The first stop on the hallway to the right was the powder room.

The door was open but the light was off. I flicked it on and saw white marble with a black and white checkered tile floor. Again, everything was spotless. I turned the light off, and walked down the hallway to two more open doorways. Peeking inside, I saw a guest bedroom, empty, and a master bedroom, also empty. The master bedroom had a spacious bathroom with a giant soaking tub, but no Barry Kemp.

Hmmm.

Back through the kitchen I went, to a door that opened into the garage. A silver Mercedes was parked inside. Other than the car, the garage was completely empty. No storage.

No gardening tools. Nothing. It didn't even smell like a garage.

Only one door remained, and I knew that would be down to the basement. There was no upstairs as it was a low-slung modern ranch house. But in Michigan, every house had a basement.

I opened the door and was conditioned to smell what every basement usually offers the olfactory senses: a combination of moisture, dank air and mold.

Not Barry Kemp's.

It was a blend of potpourri, bleach and something metallic. As I descended the stairs, the metallic scent became stronger and as the first set of weightlifting equipment came into view, my suspicions were confirmed. The metallic odors came from weights and—

Barry Kemp's body.

Or, more accurately, what was left of it.

The poor bastard had been torn apart in what could only have been a murderous frenzy. His main torso was hanging from a pull-up bar while chunks of flesh and body parts were scattered around like some sort of nightmarish anatomic puzzle. The walls were covered with blood splatter and for a brief moment I tried to match the strips of bloody flesh with what part of the body it may have come from.

I was unsuccessful.

A waft of blood, shit and bodily fluid washed over me and I backed out of the room, tripped over a leather weightlifting belt and retraced my steps and went out through the front door.

Time to call Ellen and 911, in that order.

In the meantime, I felt shock and the urge to vomit, but I held it in check. I'd never seen such carnage, except in the movies.

As I made the call to Ellen, my hand was shaking.

CHAPTER TWENTY-TWO

His name was Ron Majewski. The correct, Polish pronunciation was to say "Ma-yef-ski," but he had long ago stopped correcting people who liked to pronounce the "jew" part as you might expect.

His title was Patrolman Ron Majewski, and he worked in the area known as District 7, which also bordered the "downtown services" portion of Detroit proper. The shift was almost over when he got a radio call about a possible deceased person floating in the Detroit River.

The dispatcher told him the general area and it turned out to be on Belle Isle, the tiny spit of land in the middle of the Detroit River, just north of the city.

There were several places on Belle Isle where the water was accessible from land, and Patrolman Majewski wondered exactly how the body had been spotted and more importantly, how long it would take the coroner to get out there and bag it. If it was a complex affair requiring help with a boat, the whole process could take way longer than he wanted it to, because his shift was supposed to end in an hour and he really wanted to get home.

He'd recorded the new Quentin Tarantino western and he couldn't wait to watch it. He'd grown up watching shoot-em-up westerns and was happy they were making a comeback.

Majewski turned onto Belle Isle, and drove until he spotted another cop car ahead, pulled over just past one of the small footbridges that spanned various branches of the river.

Majewski parked the car, got out and joined the other cop on the footbridge.

"Terry, what do we have?" he asked him. The cop was Paul Terry, a muscular African-American cop Majewski knew more by reputation than anything else. He was not a man to be trifled with.

"Looks like we got some sharks in the Detroit River," Terry answered. He pointed his flashlight beam over the bridge into the water and Majewski let out a low whistle. The vague shape of a man was visible, but it appeared he'd been savagely torn apart by something, or someone.

"We're gonna need a bigger boat," Majewski said. "I'll never put on a life jacket." Jaws was one of his all-time favorite movies. If he was channel surfing and it was on, he was almost powerless to stop himself from watching and then, like now, he would quote dialogue from the movie for days afterward.

"What are you talking about?" Terry looked at him with scorn. "Let's see if we can make our way down there. Coroner is on the way."

"Who found him?" Majewski asked as he followed Terry to the end of the footbridge, off the walking path, and into the weeds that led down to the small channel. It was nothing more than a tiny inlet from the river. There was no current and the water was stagnant.

Clearly, the corpse hadn't been washed in here by the river. Majewski figured someone dropped him from the bridge, in fact, probably from the exact spot where they'd just been standing.

"Hope this isn't poison ivy," he said as he tore through some thick weeds.

"Shit, this is a mess," Terry said ahead of him. Majewski caught up to the other cop and they both looked at the remains of the body before them.

Majewski could just make out the vague shape of a torso, but the rest of it reminded him of the meat displays at Eastern Market. One chunk was definitely a leg, he could tell that by the high top basketball shoe it was still wearing.

"When someone tears a body up like that, doesn't it usually indicate they knew them?" Majewski asked his fellow cop. "The more violence inflicted on the body, the greater the likelihood the killer knew them personally?"

Even in the dark, Majewski could see Terry's raised eyebrow.

"What, you been watchin' Silence of the Lambs again?"

Majewski felt his face go red with heat, but he knew he was right. He had read that somewhere.

The body shifted in the water and Majewski gave an involuntary start until he realized Terry had merely poked it with the end of his baton.

"Scared you, didn't I?" Terry said, without turning around.

Majewski didn't answer but instead looked down at the body. The part that seemed to indicate a face had turned slightly up from the water and he couldn't stop looking at him. Something tugged at his brain, an image he couldn't quite place.

The chunk of flesh was definitely part of a face. Majewski could tell that because he could make out the shape of an eye.

And then it hit him.

"Jesus, I might know who this is," he said, as his mind ran through the catalog of faces every cop had stored in his brain. Witnesses, confidential informants, thugs, suspects. The parade of personalities flashed through Majewski's mind. And then suddenly, one separated itself from the others.

"Flowers," he said. No, that wasn't quite right. "He's a homeless guy. Used to be a big-shot lawyer."

"His lawyerin' days are over," Terry said.

"Flores!" Majewski exclaimed. "Angelo Flores. A homeless guy I rousted a few times."

"Are you ass clowns done fucking up my crime scene?" a voice called from the bridge overhead.

They both looked up and recognized the medical examiner so they made their way back up to where the forensics team was assembling their gear to retrieve the body.

The coroner was a slim white man with big glasses. He looked like a high school librarian and when he saw Terry's massive body emerge from the dense brush, he suddenly realized who he had just cursed. And just as suddenly, he got very busy.

Majewski shared his hunch on the identity of the corpse with the coroner, as well as the pair of detectives who eventually made their way to the scene. Majewski was quite proud of himself. He didn't plan on being a patrolman his whole life, and little things like this were noted in his file. In fact, he made a mental note to go home and right down his contribution to the case so he could whip it out during his next performance evaluation.

He spent the next hour watching the body being removed from the water and eventually hauled away.

It wasn't exactly how he had anticipated his shift ending, but that was the great thing about being a cop. You never knew what the hell your day was going to turn out to be.

He thought again of the Jaws movie.

"He's gone under the boat," Majewski said to the silence in his squad car. "He's gone under the boat!"

CHAPTER TWENTY-THREE

"You're not making me happy," Ellen said.

We were standing outside of Barry Kemp's house. There were at least four squad cars, as well as the coroner's vehicle, and a news van had appeared on the scene. Ellen and I were leaning against her squad car, using it to block the view of the news people.

"Hey, it's not my fault. He was dead when I got here," I said.

"Why didn't you tell me he called you?"

"He said he wanted to hire me, not that he had any new evidence," I said, which wasn't exactly a lie. He said he had information, not evidence. Big difference.

"Run through it for me again," she said. I stopped myself from rolling my eyes. My sister wanted me to tell her the story again to see if there were any kind of inconsistencies, like I was an amateur.

She was just doing her job, though, so I told her the same story, start to finish, without adding any new details, mostly because there wasn't anything else.

"Right," she said, with about as much enthusiasm as a bald man realizing he's having a mid-life crisis.

Ellen went over and joined a group of cops and a detective who had already questioned me. They had my statement and I was free to go, but I wanted to hang around. Something was terribly wrong with this whole scenario and as it continued to nag at me, I found myself not wanting to drive back to Grosse Pointe. I was missing something and it was staring me right in the face.

Ellen walked back over to me.

"Do me a favor," she said. "Leave."

So much for waiting for inspiration to strike.

"I understand, those guys over there are threatened by me," I said. "Happens all the time, so many men with low self-esteem. It's an epidemic."

Ellen had already started walking back into Kemp's house and ignored me.

Because of her oh-so-subtle suggestion, I left too and went back to my car, got inside and turned the key. I sat there for a minute or two, still trying to figure out what was nagging me.

My phone buzzed and I figured it was Anna wondering where the hell I was. I hadn't really had time to tell her what was going on and now it had gotten late. She probably wouldn't be too happy when she heard I was in Royal Oak again and I didn't plan on telling her I'd stumbled into a murder scene.

With a tap of the thumb I unlocked my screen and the phone came to life. I saw that I had several new text messages. I clicked on the messages icon and suddenly I was looking at a woman's back, bent over in front of me, with her buttocks being actively penetrated by someone's member, not mine.

Porn?

What the hell?

My first thought was that I'd been spammed, but how had they gotten my phone number?

I looked again at the photo. It was clearly shot from the man's point of view and I realized he was the one who'd snapped the photo.

My next thought was panic. Porn on my phone! I suddenly felt like a seventh-grader who'd been caught hiding a Penthouse under his mattress.

Who the hell had sent this to me? It had no return contact, just a jumble of numbers.

Another message from the same sender was waiting for me. I groaned inwardly and clicked on it, actually holding the phone farther away from me, as if the image would be less offensive.

Porn again, this time the woman was on her back with her legs spread, but her face was covered.

"Jesus," I said. A million thoughts raced through my mind.

The third and final message from the sender awaited me. I let out a deep breath and tapped.

Oral sex, this time, which at least showed the woman's face.

A little gasp from my mouth echoed in the car.

It was Judy Platkin.

CHAPTER TWENTY-FOUR

My first instinct was to delete the pornographic photos. I mean, come on, as a husband and a Dad the last thing I want to be doing is carrying around a bunch of smut on my phone.

Call me old-fashioned, but old habits die hard.

However, it was now evidence. Evidence of what, was the question. Evidence that Judy Platkin was into porn? Because that's what it looked like to me. She knew she was being filmed. In the oral shot, her eyes were locked onto the photographer. This was no hidden camera – unless the guy was wearing a spy camera around his chest, which seemed unlikely.

This felt like one of those porn cases that usually happens with celebrities. A consensual sex tape that is eventually made public, stolen from a Hollywood A-Lister by their plumber.

Had some contractor grabbed a homemade sex tape from a well-to-do Grosse Pointe woman and made it public? But why send it to me?

The person who'd sent me these lovely images had carefully concealed their identity. Somehow, a phone number didn't show up on the display, rather, all that appeared was a jumble of letters and digits.

How had they managed that? I'd never heard of anyone even being able to do that.

There was a person who could help me with that, though, so I forwarded the sender contact, not the porn, to Chi Chi. Maybe she could use some of her computer wizardry to figure out where the messages had actually originated.

That done, I put the car in gear and pointed it back toward Grosse Pointe.

Frankly, I was glad to get away from the carnage I'd seen at Barry Kemp's house. I'd seen death before, certainly, but not quite in that graphic of a situation. I mean, that was a killing frenzy.

Traffic was light and I was soon close to my exit from the freeway. As I pulled off the Interstate, it occurred to me that I knew where Judy Platkin lived. She had hosted a party a few years back and for some reason or the other, Anna and I had been on the invite list and we went. Ordinarily I would never remember such a detail, but that party always stood out to me because the Platkins actually ran out of booze and one woman was so desperate for more that she called home and had her teenage daughter bring a bunch of bottles to the Platkins. That, my friend, was a very real need for alcohol.

The Platkins lived on a street called Yorkshire in a big house made with yellow brick. Not bright yellow, more of a soft hue, like cat urine. I'd suggested that to Anna and she had shushed me before the party. Still, I remember walking around thinking that it actually did smell like cat piss, but that I was probably just imagining it.

The good thing was, it made it easy for me to spot the house. I pulled past it, drove down the block and then turned around. I parked a few houses down from the Platkins but knew that I couldn't stay too long in the space. Grosse

Pointers are notorious busybodies and I knew someone was probably already watching me, their hand on a phone to call the cops if I started doing something weird.

The street was quiet. A couple of cars passed me up ahead on Kercheval, going toward the village. Other than that, it was silent.

The debate going on in my mind was fairly intense. I wanted to go up and ring the doorbell and see if Judy was home. But to what effect? I certainly had no intention of showing her photos of herself having sex with someone. I imagined myself holding the phone up and thrusting them directly into her face for maximum shock.

But something told me she wouldn't really be all that shocked.

What would I gain by questioning her? Plus, I really spent a fair amount of time trying not to be an asshole. Confronting her about an affair, with sex pictures, in her own home?

Certainly the fact that Dave was dead and she might have had something to do with it, or somehow be involved, made a case for forgetting the niceties of the moment. But still, there was probably a better way to confront her, if that's what I ultimately decided to do.

I thought about texting Anna but didn't want to use the phone in the darkened car and give the people watching from their homes a reason to call the cops on me.

Finally, I decided it was time to go.

But just as I was about to key the ignition, a motion light at the back of the Platkins' house went on and moments later, a car backed out of the driveway.

I got a good look at the driver.

It was Judy Platkin.

CHAPTER TWENTY-FIVE

The first thing I did was check my watch.

Just past eleven p.m.

Now, ordinarily that was no big deal. And I'm not about to say that everyone in Grosse Pointe is boring because that's certainly not the case.

But the idea of Judy Platkin heading out on the town at eleven p.m. was a little off. For starters, Grosse Pointe was usually winding down at that time. Plus, she was going alone. And lastly, she headed straight down to Jefferson Avenue, which was a straight shot into Detroit.

Now, the idea of meeting friends in downtown Detroit isn't unusual, but beginning the night at this time was a little odd.

So I did what seemed like a good idea.

I followed her.

It was easy, except for the fact that the road was almost completely empty. I had to hang way back but it was easy in Detroit, because everyone ignores the stoplights. There was no risk of losing her.

Eventually, I realized we were following almost the exact

same path I'd taken when I'd followed Dave's cell phone pings.

And then it got really weird.

Because she turned down the exact same street I had before, the one that I'd taken to the abandoned warehouse. By the time I turned onto the street, just moments after she'd turned from Jefferson onto St. Aubin, I expected to see a pair of bright red taillights. The same ones I'd followed down from Grosse Pointe.

But there weren't any.

Which was impossible.

This area was mostly abandoned. There was a brewpub a couple blocks over, hanging on as the sole retail business that survived the previous economic drought. But there was hardly anything else.

So where had she gone?

I gunned the car forward, whipping my head left and right at every intersection. No sign of Judy Platkin.

This was bullshit. It couldn't be. A moment ago I'd been bragging about how easy it was to tail her and now here I was looking like an asshole who'd lost her.

I circled around the block, no sign of Judy Platkin.

It seemed like an awfully big coincidence that we'd wound up here, a stone's throw from the warehouse.

That's probably where she was.

But why?

I drove down a block, and turned right, found myself quickly at the intersection where I'd parked before and done my search through the warehouse.

Now, I didn't see anything.

I rolled down the windows and shut off my car.

No sound whatsoever.

Damnit, John, I said to myself.

You lost her.

CHAPTER TWENTY-SIX

That night, I dreamt I was tied up in the warehouse with rats gnawing at my feet. Just when I was about to pass out from the pain, I heard footsteps and screamed for the person to come and save me from the rats. A figure stepped out from the shadows. It was Dave. He had a gun. He pointed the gun at the rats and then just before he shot, he tilted the gun up and shot me.

My eyes snapped open.

My body was covered in sweat and my breath was coming in fast, shallow gasps. I glanced over next to me and saw Anna was still asleep. That was good. Nothing worse than waking her up earlier than necessary.

It was early, but not so early that I needed to try to get back to sleep. So I got out of bed, made a pot of coffee, got dressed, filled a huge thermos of fresh coffee and drove to my office.

It was still early and only a few people were out and about, getting coffee and bagels.

I turned on the lights, set some soft jazz on the little sound system I had and drank my coffee.

The dream was still in my mind but I forced myself to forget it. I had work to do.

It was still a mystery to me how Judy Platkin had managed to ditch me. Where had she gone? My best guess was that she'd simply looped back, hopped onto Jefferson, and headed somewhere else. But that would mean that she had seen me behind her and then had outmaneuvered me.

Not exactly something to be proud of, as a private investigator.

My phone buzzed and I looked down at the screen.

A text message from Nate.

You up?

I typed back. *Yep, at office.*

Suddenly, my phone started a constant buzz and I picked it up.

"Did you hear about the floater down on Belle Isle?" Nate asked me. I took a drink of my coffee. Never too early to hear Nate talking crime.

"Nope."

"Some homeless guy," he said.

"Since you're calling me about it," I observed, "I assume there's more to it than just a drunk homeless guy drowning."

"Yeah, this guy was cut up pretty well," Nate said. "You might even use the term butchered."

I put down my coffee cup. Images of Barry Kemp's body filled my vision.

"It's that serial killer again," Nate said.

"I thought you told me he was killing hookers?"

"Hookers, but also a couple of homeless people. Sometimes it's hard to tell the difference, because there isn't always a difference."

"Huh," I said. The coffee hadn't kicked in yet.

"But don't tell anybody," Nate said, lowering his voice as if Herbert Hoover had installed phone taps on our lines. "There are a lot of whispers about it, the FBI is getting involved, from what I hear."

"When you say butchered, what do you mean, exactly?" I asked.

Nate let out a soft laugh. "What do you think I mean? It looked like a frenzy killing. Like someone really got into it once the blood and body parts started flying everywhere. Whoever this maniac is, he really enjoys his work."

There was a pause and I let it go on too long because Nate's reporter instincts flared up. "What?" he asked. "Do you know something? Does this relate to a case you're working on?"

I could practically picture him with his cell phone tucked under his chin, his fingers poised above his keyboard ready to take notes.

"Probably not," I said, without much conviction.

"Huh, doesn't sound like you've convinced yourself," he said.

Just then, an email popped up on my computer screen and I saw it was from Chi Chi.

"Look, I've gotta run. I'll call you if I hear anything."

I disconnected and opened up the email.

The message was done in Chi Chi's typical terse style:

Email was encrypted and used a rerouting service. But I traced it back to a chat room. You need to come over here and see this.

Having finished my first giant thermos of coffee, I refilled it, locked up my office and headed down to my car.

Chi Chi lived just north of Grosse Pointe in a suburb called St. Clair Shores.

I knew it well.

On the way, I thought about the dead body on Belle Isle and then about Barry Kemp.

There was no way they could be related.

But the description of the killing seemed awfully similar.

I vowed to keep an open mind.

When it came to the kind of killing I'd seen at Barry Kemp's place and what Nate described, I knew I wasn't dealing with someone logical.

Someone was full of rage.

CHAPTER TWENTY-SEVEN

Chi Chi's place was an anomaly, just like the woman herself. Over the years, the homes along the right side of Jefferson Avenue, the ones with frontage on Lake St. Clair, had been torn down and replaced with McMansions.

Except for Chi Chi's house.

It was an original cottage, probably built in the 1920s. Small, with wood trim and a wide, expansive yard. The open space was the biggest shock because in all of her neighbors' homes, every usable square inch of the building lot had been taken up by the new construction. Square footage was king, right? Every hour literally nearly bumped up against the next house over. You can pass salt-and-pepper shakers through the windows from one house to the next.

I parked in the driveway, behind the one-car garage. Even though Chi Chi was single, she usually had a lot of family around so I was surprised to see an empty driveway.

After a quick knock on the front door (no doorbell) it opened and I stared into the face of a much older version of Chi Chi, probably sixty years older than my former client, but with the same wide, oval face, dark eyes and sly smile.

If the woman had a name, I had no idea what it might be.

"Mama," I said.

"John," she answered. We hugged and I stepped inside, took off my shoes and accepted a cup of tea. The tiny house was always full of wonderful smells. Usually tea, mixed with some exotic spices.

"She in her office," Mama said, her voice thick with a Vietnamese accent.

I walked down the house's only hallway, turned in at the first doorway. It was a converted master bedroom, featuring a beautiful picture window that looked out on the lake. The natural light would have filled the room, if not for the blinds that were partially obscuring the view.

This was done so the tiny person behind the giant computer screens could watch the magic she was creating unfold, without glare from outside light.

Chi Pham was well under five feet tall, and I didn't even bother to hazard a guess at her weight. Sometimes she reminded me of the tiny gazelles you occasionally see on the Discovery Channel, running from cheetahs.

But this one didn't run from anyone.

When I'd helped clear her in the bogus lawsuit her former employer tried to bring, I practically had to hold her back.

"What kind of crap are you into now?" she asked. She swiveled in her giant office chair – a monstrosity made of brown leather, the kind you usually imagine a judge from the 1800s would be using. Her feet dangled, and her body left tons of room on each side. You could have fit three of her into that chair.

"The usual crap," I said. "The John Rockne kind of crap we all know and love."

"Uh-huh," she said. "You hungry? Want Mama to make up something?"

"No, that's okay," I said. "I've got a stomach full of coffee, and now tea."

Chi Chi leaned back in her chair and put her feet up on the desk. She was wearing a pair of throwback Nike sneakers. Probably size 3.

As I settled into the more modest chair next to her desk. I rolled over closer to her so I could see her screen, which right now had a bunch of weird letters on it. Coding, I figured. Whatever the hell that meant.

"First off, you had asked me to look into lawsuits regarding Barry, or Bertram, Kemp. I've found nothing so far, at least that I can make sense of. I need another couple of days."

"Okay," I said. "And I want to pay you for your help."

She ignored me. "So what was attached to these messages that were sent to you?" she asked. And then, "No! Let me guess. Something sexual."

Her little almond face, with the large, expressive eyes beamed back at me, full of mischief.

"Yeah, something like that," I said, picturing the main image of Judy Platkin orally servicing someone.

"That's what I thought," she said.

"And what led you to that conclusion?"

Chi Chi laughed. "You know I have to show you what I did, right? I can't just tell you, that's no fun."

I was tempted to say that having fun wasn't exactly the objective here, but since she was doing me a favor, I let her have her moment.

She swung her feet back down and they dangled, at least six inches from the ground.

"Okay, I already told you it was encrypted, but not very well," Chi Chi explained. She tapped a key on her keyboard and the scrambled jumble of letters reshaped themselves into actual words.

"Still, there was one more hurdle," she said. I peered at

the screen. There were words, but they didn't make any sense. It read like a scrambled word puzzle.

"You see, this isn't actually content, it's asking for a password," Chi Chi said. "It was fairly well disguised because if you didn't know what you were looking at, you would assume it was a message."

She then carefully highlighted certain letters in the mix of words, hit the return key, and everything vanished momentarily until a new screen popped up.

I recognized the form.

It was a chat room.

The rooms had ominous labels:

Mrs. X's.
   Swingers.
   Pegs.
   G-Master.
   G. Licky
   TeamBottom.
   Gold Back Door.
   NoLimit.

"What the hell is this?" I asked.

Chi Chi laughed.

"Oh, my little innocent private investigator," she said. "You really have to get out more, John."

"Sex?" I asked.

She nodded. "The real naughty stuff," she said, a wickedly sly smile appearing on her face. "Bondage. S & M. Partner swapping." She peered closely at me. "Are you into this kind of stuff?"

"Oh sure," I said. "Anna and I love spanking each other

and strangers whenever we get the chance."

Chi Chi grunted. "Yeah, right."

She tapped some more keys. "There's not much really here to show you. It looks like users pop in, exchange messages and leave. It's not a very robust interface and there's no way to trace the identities of the people participating."

"Other than the sex stuff, did you see anything strange?"

"Yeah, the traffic is low. Like, really low. It makes me wonder if this is something else. If it serves a different purpose."

I puzzled over that and then filed it away.

Well, it made sense. It would seem that the person who sent me the porno pictures of Judy Platkin, probably was involved in this sex chat room somehow.

And then a crazy idea hit me.

"So this is a chat room, right?" I asked.

Chi Chi moved her head side-to-side. "Not quite," she said. "It does function partially as that, but it looks like there was a calendar, some obscure references to other groups and even a web cam option although I haven't been able to figure out how that works."

"So correct me if I'm wrong," I said, thinking out loud. "These kinds of people, they don't have sex together online, right?"

"Well, the web cam people do."

"Ok, but are they all doing it via web cam? Wouldn't that get boring after awhile. How do you spank someone virtually?"

"That's a fair point," Chi Chi said.

"You said there is a calendar, right?"

"No, I said there *was* a calendar."

I looked at her, confused.

Chi Chi sighed. "Do you know how Google will often cache things that were posted online?"

I vaguely remembered how that worked, but she interpreted my pause as if I didn't understand her.

"Basically, if I post something and then delete it right away, Google remembers the post and will cache it," she explained. "This chat room I'm showing you isn't live anymore. Someone wiped the whole thing clean. But I found a way to find the cached version, and believe me, it wasn't on Google. It took a lot of digging on my part. By tomorrow, you won't even be able to find this version anymore, which is why I took a lot of screen grabs for you."

My head was spinning a little bit.

"Can you tell when it was deleted?"

"Sure," Chi Chi said. "Last night, just before midnight."

Right after Judy Platkin gave me the slip downtown.

"Why did you ask about the calendar?" Chi Chi said.

It was just a hunch, but I had a feeling I was right. "Well, these people need to get together to really do their thing, right?"

"I believe that's how anatomy works."

And then, out of the blue, another thought struck me. The homeless guy near Ford Field. What had he said? I desperately thought back and then suddenly, I had it. He'd said something about crazy white people and them being half-naked.

"So if they had a calendar, this website or whatever the hell it was, might have been more like a virtual club that was kind of like a gateway to a real club."

"Could be," Chi Chi conceded.

It made a lot of sense to me, too.

And I figured I knew the perfect location for a clandestine sex club.

It would be in a warehouse district devoid of people.

Like the one where Judy Platkin had mysteriously disappeared.

CHAPTER TWENTY-EIGHT

Since my main job was to stick my nose in everybody else's business, I figured my sister might as well be next.

"Put me through to the Chief of Police, please," I said. "This is the Ferrari dealership and we have some news regarding the new car she ordered."

Silence filled the other end of the line until I heard Ellen's voice.

"What do you want, John? I'm busy with a homicide case if you'd forgotten."

"Well, ironically, that's why I was calling. Did you find out anything at Barry Kemp's place?"

Another patch of silence and then I heard Ellen's door shut.

"Why should I tell you?" she said. "I haven't gotten shit for my offer of collaboration. And now you want me to feed you information?"

"I've got some stuff, but I figured you would want to go first. As I remember from my childhood you just always had to be first."

"Cute," she said. "Well, we did discover one minor detail."

"What's that?"

"It seems the body parts at Barry Kemp's didn't come from Barry Kemp."

"What?" For a second I thought she might be screwing with me, but I knew her too well.

"Whose were they?"

"No idea," she said. "We've got the blood out to the lab and told them to put a rush on it. But while the body did belong to a male, the dental records definitely did not match Barry Kemp's. And while I know what a hardened investigator you are, you somehow missed that the arm found near the corner had none of the musculature definition Barry Kemp is so proud of."

Now I was embarrassed again. How had I missed that?

Because I didn't look, that's why. The carnage was so extensive and I was worried about contaminating the crime scene.

"And don't try to tell me you didn't want to contaminate the crime scene," she said, reading my mind and beating me to the punch. "You ran out of there like a scared little bunny."

The bunny reference always got to me.

"Well, I've got some information for you," I countered.

"Shocker."

"It seems there's a sex club of some sort that has something to do with this case. I just haven't found out how." I filled her in on my trip downtown, to the warehouse and my encounter with the homeless guy by Ford Field. Since she was the reason I had followed Dave's cell phone locations around the city, I knew she couldn't get mad at me for making some assumptions.

"That's all you've got?" Ellen asked. "Why didn't I realize I'd be getting the raw end of this deal?"

"I'm assuming that's a rhetorical question."

"Try to do some better detective work, John, or don't call me again."

Just when she was about to hang up and I was sure I would be talking to a dead phone line, she added something.

"Oh, by the way. Barry Kemp's lawyer, a guy named Gadlicke, said he would only talk to you. You're supposed to call him ASAP."

Now I heard the disconnect.

It always amazed me that we were brother and sister. I mean, I am who I am.

And she's a total pain in the ass.

CHAPTER TWENTY-NINE

A lawyer wanting to talk to me. That never sounded good. Somehow I felt like a kid being called to the principal's office.

I called and got a same-day appointment, which made me a little nervous. Usually high-powered attorneys have schedules backed up for weeks. Or maybe he was just anxious to talk to me.

This case was putting a few miles on my car, I thought, as I headed out to Bloomfield Hills, the rolling bluffs full of giant, sprawling homes, luxury cars in winding driveways and the smell of investment bankers in the air.

At an intersection I saw a modern office building, probably built in the 1980s, that showed no signs of any attempted remodeling. I pictured people in polyester, smoking cigarettes and snorting coke in the bathroom.

There was an empty space near the front door. In fact, there were a lot of empty spaces. Either Gadlicke's law firm wasn't the kind that generated a lot of foot traffic, or the firm had seen better times.

Which surprised me, because when I searched the web, it

had looked like he had a team of fifteen lawyers, and covered all kinds of areas, including medical malpractice.

What, I thought, *something wasn't true on the Internet? Shocking.*

Inside the building, I caught a whiff of old people and stale coffee.

The elevator doors were covered with a faux wood pattern and I heard them at least two floors before they actually arrived. When the doors opened, it sounded like an audio clip of a submarine being sunk by a torpedo.

Inside, I gave my odds of getting to the seventh floor about fifty-fifty.

As luck would have it, I made the trip. The doors banged open and I jumped out of the death trap with a plan to take the stairs down after my meeting.

There was only one hallway leading to one door on the floor, so I followed it to the sign that read Gadlicke & Associates. The brass-plated door handle turned under my hand and I pushed my way inside.

The lobby was a wall of dark green carpet, office chairs that looked like they belonged in a dentist's office decorated thirty years ago, and a plywood reception desk that resembled a bar in a bankrupt pool hall.

There was a hallway that went around the desk and there must have been a silent door alarm because a guy suddenly appeared at the desk.

He didn't look like your average receptionist.

More accurately, he looked like an offensive linemen in the NFL. Easily standing 6'5" or so, way over three hundred pounds, all of it stuffed into a suit that looked like it was from the Wal-Mart Office Collection. It was a jarring sight.

Why in the hell did Barry Kemp choose this place for his law firm?

"I'm here to see Mr. Gadlicke," I said, realizing I didn't have a first name.

Dead silence. He looked at me and I felt like he was staring at me like I was a mosquito on his arm, deciding if it was worth the effort to squash me.

He turned without saying a word and disappeared down the hallway. I could actually feel the vibrations as his mass rumbled deeper into the office.

After several minutes where one of the recessed lights above me blinked out, I again felt the earth's tremors and it reminded me of the scene in Jurassic Park where the puddle of water started getting ripples every time the T-Rex was about to appear.

"Mr. Gadlicke will see you," he said.

"I'm excited," I replied. I walked past the plywood reception desk, which I noticed had no phone, pens or paper. I made a hard left at the Human Tower of Meat and walked down the hallway.

I heard no people talking, saw no one, perceived absolutely no sign of life until I got to the last office at the end of the hall.

There was a desk with a man seated behind it, surrounded by four chairs, all occupied.

Two of the chairs each barely contained a man the same size and muscle mass as my escort.

The third chair held a thin, pale, freckled man with curly orange hair. He looked like the comedian Carrot Top after a hunger strike.

Behind the desk was, I assumed, Mr. Gadlicke. He was also thin, with an enormous Adam's apple, thinning, slicked back salt-and-pepper hair, thick glasses and he was dressed in a black suit with a thin black tie. He looked like an out-of-work undertaker from an Old West television show.

"Mr. Rockne," Gadlicke said.

"Hello everybody," I said.

"Let me be brief," Gadlicke said. "You're here because the police are looking into the disappearance of my client, Mr. Barry Kemp. Mr. Kemp informed me that he had hired you to look into the murder of David Ingells, is that correct?"

Gadlicke's voice was harsh, as in a I-smoke-three-cartons-of-cigarettes-every-morning kind of harsh.

"No, he did not hire me," I said gently. "He said he *wanted* to hire me. But before we could draw up a contract someone made a meat salad out of him."

I looked around the room at the others, but they were all watching me, like I was an object of curiosity.

"As his attorney, I am authorized to finalize that agreement," Gadlicke continued. "Please consider yourself hired as of right now."

For a moment, I was at a loss of words. Gadlicke seemed to take it as a bargaining tactic.

"At double your normal rate." He flourished a batch of papers and one of the giant slabs of beef brought it to me. It did, in fact, show a contract with twice my normal fee, signed by Gadlicke, along with a check.

It occurred to me to look at the walls to see Gadlicke's diploma. I was curious where he'd gone to law school. I looked around, but the only thing framed on the wall was a horrible painting of George Washington.

"That's the normal ten percent you require up front, correct?" Gadlicke asked me. His eyes flicked over my shoulder to the painting, and I wondered if he was its creator.

I nodded.

"What—"

"Your job," he interrupted me, "is to do what Mr. Kemp originally asked, but I have one small addendum. In addition to finding out the killer of Mr. Ingells, I want you to locate Mr. Kemp. Please report back to me, here, in exactly 48 hours. And I should tell you, Mr. Rockne, I expect you to do a thoroughly satisfactory job. I don't like to be disappointed."

"But–"

My elbow was grabbed and I was pulled out of the office. The door shut quickly behind me.

With Sasquatch behind me, I marched out of the office, down the stairs and out to my car.

Huh, I thought.

Ten percent down? I never asked for that, but it seemed like a good idea.

CHAPTER THIRTY

Something was gnawing at me again, like a beaver attacking a sapling.

I'd worked plenty of cases before, but this one was really getting under my skin, maybe because I knew Dave so well and he was a friend. Maybe my emotions were getting in the way of clear thinking.

Or maybe I was just making a bunch of excuses for my lack of progress.

Whatever the deal was, as I drove down Woodward Avenue, headed for the freeway back to Grosse Pointe, I knew I was missing something.

I turned on the radio, plugged in my phone and listened to some Black Keys as I drove. Their driving beat blues music always put me into a cool groove.

As I drove, I couldn't get over the goofy meeting with Gadlicke.

What the hell was that about? And did I really want to cash his check? Something told me that would be a really bad idea.

The guy gave me the creeps and I had to believe he wasn't

Kemp's real lawyer. I mean, Dave's practice was highly successful. A good law firm would be essential. So why was Kemp working with a slimeball-looking guy like Gadlicke? And what was the deal with the hired muscle? Would a legit law firm need so much security?

Suddenly, my mind ratcheted back to my meeting with Chi Chi. *Holy shit.*

I turned off the music and speed dialed her.

"What's up, John?" she asked. "I'm playing cat-and-mouse with a Russian hacker. He's good. But not good enough."

"Hey, something's bothering me."

"Try an itch cream, that should help for that area."

"Funny. No, what were the names of the rooms in that sex chat room? I think I missed something."

I heard the tapping of keys.

"Funny you should ask, I have something for you."

A car careened in front of me, driven by an old man whose head could barely be seen above the steering wheel. With a swerve around him, I gunned it onto the entrance ramp for the freeway.

"Here they are," she read. "Mrs. X's. Swingers. Pegs. G-Master. G. Licky. TeamBottom. NoLimit."

"Yes!" I shouted inside the car. "G. Licky. Gladlicke. No way that's a coincidence."

"Speaking of coincidences," Chi Chi said. "I've got another one for you."

My mind was going full tilt and I barley heard her. If Gladlicke was tied to Judy Platkin, who was possibly tied to Dave, and Dave was connected to Kemp, who also was linked to Gladlicke...

"I have two tidbits of information for you," Chi Chi said, interrupting my internal brainstorm. "Number one, you asked me to look into pending lawsuits regarding Barry, or Bertram Kemp."

"Yes, that's right."

"Well, I didn't find anything officially. However, you know what the dark web is, correct?"

"Sure, it's the part of the Internet not visible to the public. Like, websites that even the search engines don't know about."

"Right, and do you know what the currency of the dark web is?"

"I think I do but I can't remember."

"It's called Bitcoin," Chi Chi said patiently.

"Okay."

"Don't ask me how but I found myself inside Barry Kemp's private email and I found some bitcoin transactions," she said, her voice the picture of innocence. "Fairly large payments mostly around $10,000 or so."

"Payments *to* Kemp or *from* him?"

"To him."

"Okay. So somebody was paying him for something and doing it with bitcoin through the dark web."

"Right."

I ran that through my brain.

"While I was in there, I found some messages from his Webmaster," she said. "At least, I thought it was his Webmaster."

"You mean, for his medical website?"

"Yes, that's what I initially thought. But then I realized it wasn't for his medical site."

Something clicked into place.

"It was for the sex chat room," I said.

"Exactly. And it wasn't a Webmaster," she said.

Another tumbler clicked into place.

"The G-Master room on the sex site," I said, practically shouting.

"You got it," she said. And then her voice became almost

somber. "But I'm afraid I have some bad news for you."

Dread filled my stomach.

"The G-Master's messages came from a personal account," she explained. "I was able to trace it to a person.

"Who?" I asked, but I felt like I already knew the answer.

"Dave Ingells."

CHAPTER THIRTY-ONE

As much as I tried, as an objective professional investigator, I just couldn't wrap my brain around Dave being involved in some sort of online sex club, most likely with a physical counterpart somewhere in downtown Detroit.

It was ridiculous.

Out of the question.

Preposterous.

But still...

Anna had told me about the rumor of Dave porking Judy Platkin. Yes, I believe 'porking' was the exact word she used.

Anna.

My plan had been to go back to the office, but now, I wanted to go home and talk to my wife. Who had told her that rumor? How long ago? Where? I vaguely remembered her mentioning a friend named Fran, but I think Fran had just been the host of the gathering.

I kicked myself for not being more aggressive in following up with her on the rumor, but as I thought back to it, she had claimed nothing else. That's all she knew. And frankly, I thought the idea was so ludicrous that I had at least partially dismissed it from any serious consideration.

Until now.

Now, everything had changed.

When I got home, I grabbed a beer from the fridge, saw Anna and the girls in the family room watching a movie. Something with a princess because I could see some former well-known actress dressed in glitter with a magic wand.

After hugs and a quick chat about school, I nodded Anna toward the living room.

"Thank you," she said. "God that movie was boring." She took a drink of my beer and handed it back to me.

"How was your day?" she asked.

I flopped onto the couch and she stood, stretching.

"This case has really taken some weird turns, especially with regard to Judy Platkin," I said.

She raised an eyebrow and sat on the edge of the couch, took another drink of my beer.

"Really? Like how?"

"Let's just say she's been linked to some weird stuff, and possibly Dave, too," I said. "Which is why I wanted to ask you about that rumor. Where did you hear it? And who said it?"

She shook her head. "No, I don't remember. It was just a bunch of women sitting around shooting the breeze. There have always been rumors about Judy."

"Wait, go back. So the rumor started in a group setting?"

Anna closed her eyes and sighed. "I think so. I don't know."

"I should hypnotize you," I said and then glanced back at the room where the girls were watching their movie. "And then have my way with you."

"Plus, there was wine involved," she said, ignoring me.

"A-ha, now we're getting somewhere." Anna always had a

busy social calendar full of get-togethers over coffee, lunch, dinner or drinks. Narrowing it down to a wine outing was a good first step.

"For real, John? I don't remember who said it. I think it was at Fran's house, but I can't be sure."

I thought about my options. They weren't all that great.

"Mom! You're missing a good part!" one of the girls called out. Anna stood up. "Oh gosh, some Mom jobs are worse than others."

She left me there and I pulled out my cell phone, tapped on Nate's contact icon.

"What's up?" he asked.

"What are you doing?"

"On my way home, about two blocks from your house. Are you drinking a beer?" he asked, apparently able to hear with supernatural ability the little drink I took while he was answering.

"Yeah, why?"

I waited, but didn't hear an answer, and then suddenly there were lights in my driveway. Back into the kitchen I went, set my empty beer on the counter and grabbed two more. Nate appeared on the porch and I opened the door.

"Hey," he said.

"Cheers," I replied.

Knowing my friend, I grabbed a big bowl and dumped a bunch of potato chips into it.

We each took up a spot at the kitchen table. Nate drank half his beer in one gulp. I went and grabbed him another one.

"Got some news for you on that floater," Nate said.

"Oh yeah?"

I took a peek toward the family room to make sure the girls weren't listening. Anna hated when I talked shop and the girls could hear. Especially when it was graphic.

"Had AIDS," Nate said. "Remember the serial killer I told you about? Turns out all of his victims had some kind of blood disease. Which makes perfect sense since some of them were hookers. Detroit hookers are crawling with HIV. Everyone knows that. That's why they're such easy prey."

"So you don't think it's a coincidence? That they all have some kind of disease? Seems like if you rounded up all of the prostitutes and homeless people in Detroit, there'd be a pretty high number of them infected with something."

"Maybe," Nate admitted. "But there's something there, I know it."

I hadn't really called Nate to talk about his case. I was more interested in laying out where I was. It was a lot of evidence and I wanted to spitball some theories.

"Well, I've got some news, too." I laid it all out for him. The chat room, Kemp's disappearance and possible link to Dave. It took me quite awhile and by the time I was done, both of our beers were empty, a problem I resolved with two fresh ones.

"The way you described the murder victim at Barry Kemp's, that sounds like how some of these serial killer victims were murdered."

"I thought about that, but that seems like a stretch. I'll mention it to Ellen, maybe she can pull some forensics for comparison."

"Keep me posted," Nate said, with a seriousness I understood. This was a good story and would generate a lot of clicks on his websites.

There was a pause and then we both started tossing out some theories, fueled in no small part by the alcohol.

"Maybe Dave and Barry were partners," Nate said. "A lover's spat."

"No," I said. "No way."

Nate rolled his eyes. I was breaking the rules of a brain-storming session.

"Try this," I said. "I don't think Dave was cheating on his wife, but I'll throw out this scenario just for laughs. Dave and Judy are having an affair. Barry finds out, tries to blackmail him."

"So how does Dave end up dead?" Nate asked. "With Dave dead, Barry doesn't get paid."

Nate held up a finger. "Judy Platkin's husband finds out she's sleeping with Kemp and/or Dave. He gets jealous and kills Dave."

I shook my head. "Judy's separated. The husband lives in Houston now, probably driven out by the rumors."

Nate shoveled some potato chips into his mouth and still tried to talk. "How have I never heard of this Gadlicke character? He sounds like a hoot. And Carrot Top? That's awesome."

"A really skinny Carrot Top," I corrected. "And yeah, I want to find out who that was, goddamnit."

Nate pushed away the bowl of chips. It was empty. He chugged the rest of his beer and let out a long belch, merci-fully he lowered the volume on it so the girls didn't hear.

"You know what I think?" he said.

"No, I'm still reeling from your belch's blowback."

He pointed a thick finger at me.

"If you find out who was banging Judy Platkin, you find out who killed Dave."

CHAPTER THIRTY-TWO

Sleep was one of my most favorite things in the world. Sleep and pillows. I loved pillows. I need at least four. One for my head, one between my legs, one to hug and one just in case I lose one over the side of the bed.

I used to have a dog that would spend ten minutes arranging its blanket before it would finally flop down and go to sleep. Its name was Charlie. Sometimes when I'm arranging my pillows, Anna will say, 'All set Charlie'?

Anyway, I was deep into a dream where Judy Platkin was making a porn movie and I was the director, telling her to do the scene again because I didn't feel she was properly motivated, when my cell phone buzzed on the night table.

Anna's elbow found its way into my side, with a fair amount of force.

My eyes creaked open and the porn set disappeared. I was in my bedroom. My phone was ringing.

After some fumbling around, knocking my Kindle onto the ground, I finally was able to grab the phone.

I swiped to answer, without looking at the caller.

"Help, John!" a voice screamed at me from the phone. "He's drunk and he's going to kill me!"

I pulled the phone away from my ear and looked at the screen. Carrie Barnes, wife of Adam Barnes, the violent drunk.

"Okay, what—"

But the call had ended.

Shit.

I swung my feet out of bed, threw on some clothes and ran out to the car. The thought occurred to me to call 911, but I hesitated. Carrie had called me, probably because she didn't want the embarrassment of having half a dozen Grosse Pointe cops putting on a light show in her driveway.

My gun was still locked in my safe at the office, which after some thought, I decided might be for the best. I didn't want to shoot Adam Barnes, but I realized I might be in for some sort of violent confrontation.

Shit.

It was still completely dark outside and I banged the back door open, lumbered down the back steps and got into my car.

A better option than calling the police would be to send Ellen a quick text that I was going to Carrie Barnes's house for an emergency. I had no idea if she would be awake or not, but at least someone would know where I was.

I threw the car into gear and backed out of the driveway, swung onto Kercheval and headed toward the Barnes house.

Driving and texting wasn't too dangerous because there wasn't anyone on the roads. With cell phone in hand I began thumbing a text to Ellen.

I was halfway through it when I heard a squeal of tires, followed by a loud crash and I was instantly thrown forward and my air bag exploded. The phone flew from my hand and my car veered off and hit the curb and somehow I managed to slam on the brakes to avoid driving into someone's picture window.

What happened? I was in a fog. Did I hit somebody? I hadn't even seen another car on the road, then again it was still pitch black.

My head snapped around and I saw a man with a gun outside my door lifting his arm to shoot. I threw myself down toward the passenger's footspace and clawed at the door handle as a series of insanely loud explosions rattled my already foggy brain. I felt a searing pain and then the door opened and I spilled out onto someone's grass but I instinctively rolled back under the car just in case the shooter was coming around.

Goddamnit, I thought. Why didn't I carry a gun at all times? I thought briefly of Anna and the girls still back at home in bed. And I wondered if the shooter was coming around now to finish me off.

I squirmed and looked under the car, trying to see if a pair of feet was circling around either side. I shimmied again, further under the car, and in a panic, desperately tried to see where the gunman was.

I didn't see anything.

Suddenly, I heard the slam of a car door and tires squealing, an engine racing and then everything was quiet, except for my ragged breathing.

Was it a trick? Was there more than one shooter? I waited. My face was on the pavement and I could see shards of glass in the street. If the shooter was walking around, I would have heard him. I checked both sides of the car, as well as the front and back as best I could. Since I was under the car, I didn't have much room.

Finally, I decided to risk it and I slid back out from under the car and staggered to my feet. Blood was pouring down my left arm and I felt dizzy.

There was no other car in the street.

I was alone.

Peering inside my car, I couldn't see my phone. For a brief moment, I wondered if I was still in bed having a nightmare, because it seemed like no one had heard the crash or the shots.

It was surreal.

Had it actually happened?

And then I started shaking and I realized I was actually here, not at home. This had actually happened.

Someone had tried to kill me.

I'd been set up.

Carrie Barnes had called me so someone could ambush me.

Why?

It was then that I heard a siren from not too far away. I walked over to the grass and sat down. Or, more accurately, fell down.

My head was spinning so I toppled over onto my side.

God, I missed my pillows.

CHAPTER THIRTY-THREE

"You're up way past your bedtime," Ellen said. "Anna kick you out of bed again?"

My eyes had been closed and I'd vaguely heard some cars arrive, but I hadn't bothered to see who it was. As long as they weren't here to shoot me, I was fine, which was the good news.

The bad news was, my sister had arrived on the scene.

"No, a client called and said her alcoholic husband was going to hurt her, so I was racing to the rescue, like an idiot. I drove right into an ambush."

"Who was it?" Ellen asked.

"Carrie Barnes."

A paramedic barged in between us and Ellen walked away.

After a quick inspection, the paramedic told me I hadn't been shot. It was a laceration, most likely from a shard of window glass that had sliced my arm open. A few stitches and I was all set.

The paramedic left and Ellen was back.

"Why'd she call you? You'd be the last person I would call," Ellen pointed out.

"Oh, you know Grosse Pointe."

Ellen smiled. "Yeah, I sure do. It's all about keeping up appearances, right?"

"Any word on the shooter?" I asked.

"Nope. No one saw anything. They heard the shooting, but you know how that goes."

I did. Because Grosse Pointe bordered Detroit, Grosse Pointers were used to lots of gunfire at night. Sometimes it sounded a lot closer than it actually was.

"How about you?" she asked. "What'd you see?"

"Not much," I admitted. "I saw the gun, first. And then just a shadow, really. It was dark and the muzzle flash started immediately. All I can tell you is that it was probably a male, judging by the size and shape of the silhouette."

"Marvelous." Ellen looked at me and her face was bored disappointment. "Let's get your statement, make sure the doctors are done with you, and then I'll take you home."

"That's it?" I asked. "No one saw the car that rammed me?"

"No one called. No one heard a thing," she said.

Ellen left and talked to the paramedics and then she came back.

"Let's go," she said. "I'll take you home."

"We have to make a stop first."

Ellen rolled her eyes. "The pharmacy? Need some Tylenol?"

"No. We have to go see Carrie Barnes."

On the way over, which was only a few blocks away, I filled in Ellen on the Adam Barnes situation, including the part where he threatened me if I continued to interfere with he and his family.

"Never heard of him," she said. "At least he kept his addiction under control to avoid trouble with us. Either he's not that bad, or he's just more careful than most."

"I think when he's sober he's very careful," I said. But when he's drunk, he's probably a pretty scary guy."

My head was pounding and I suddenly wished I had some Tylenol. My arms didn't feel all that great, either.

"Par for the course," she said. She looked at me. "Are you okay? You look a little pale."

Just then, the Barnes household came into view. "Here it is," I said.

Ellen pulled the squad car along the curb in front of the house. There weren't any lights on. She had called for backup, and a second squad car pulled in behind us,

"Let's go," I said.

"What do you mean?" Ellen snapped at me. "You're in no shape for this. You're waiting here."

"I've been in the house, I know the layout," I said, desperate to accompany her.

She paused and I could tell I had a good point. "Lame, but I'll let you tag along. Stay behind me." She waved to the cop in the second squad car. He got out and took up a position in the driveway.

We walked up to the house and Ellen took out her flashlight, There wasn't any signs of life inside.

She banged on the door with the butt of her flashlight.

"Hello?" she called out.

"Want me to call her?"

"Sure."

I took out my cell phone I'd managed to find inside my car and called Carrie Barnes' number. It went straight to voicemail.

"No dice," I said.

She reached in and tried the doorknob. It was unlocked.

"There's a basement to the left," I said. "The steps lead up to the kitchen and to the right is the main part of the house."

We stepped inside and Ellen pointed the flashlight up

toward the kitchen. She took a step, but then we both heard a thump from the basement.

Ellen reached out and flicked on a light switch that revealed the stairway going down, which we took.

We came around the landing and saw Carrie Barnes, hog tied on the floor with duct tape across her mouth.

CHAPTER THIRTY-FOUR

Ellen cut away the restraints and let Carrie take her own duct tape from her mouth.

"What took you so long?" Carrie screamed at me.

I was about to explain the ambush and how I'd nearly died trying to get to her, but I was interrupted.

Upstairs, we all heard the sound of feet in the hallway.

"Your kids are home?" I asked.

Ellen had stepped away and was talking into her radio. At the mention of her children, Carrie burst into tears and Ellen took the opportunity to come back and punch me in the shoulder for my insensitivity.

And yes, it was that shoulder.

I almost started crying.

"Are you okay?" Ellen asked. "Do you need medical attention? Either way, I've got an ambulance coming to check you out." She glanced at me. "They've had a busy night."

"No, I don't need anyone," Carrie said, pushing past us. We followed her up the stairs where she intercepted her daughter, and they walked back toward the bedroom.

"This is bullshit," I said. "Adam planned this. There's no

other explanation. He just happens to have a huge fight with his wife, minutes before someone just happens to crash into me and shoot up my car?"

"Why, though?" Ellen asked. "Why did he come after you? Were you still following him around?"

"No, I hadn't set eyes on him since he confronted me in my office."

We each took a chair at the Barnes' kitchen table. It was a nice house, with a terra cotta floor, gleaming white cabinets and granite countertops. Despite Adam's addiction, it looked like they were doing okay financially.

"You don't look so good," Ellen pointed out.

"Neither do you," I countered.

She laughed, just as Carrie reappeared.

"The kids are okay?" Ellen asked.

"Yes. But that asshole, that's it," she said. "I'm through with him. This was the last straw."

"What happened?" I asked.

"He was drunk again, went into a rage because I didn't have dinner ready. Which is totally ridiculous. It was almost like he wanted to fight with me and he was just looking for an excuse."

Carrie went to the sink and got herself a glass of water. I desperately wanted one, too, but didn't feel it was the right time to ask.

"That's not the worst of it," Carrie said.

She burst into tears.

Ellen looked at me out of the corner of her eye.

"What else happened, Carrie?" I prodded.

She set aside the glass of water, grabbed a wine glass and a bottle from the rack above the sink, and poured herself a huge glass of wine.

"Did he hit you?" Ellen asked.

Carrie had her back to us and I could see her small shoulders shaking as she silently cried.

"He said he was leaving me," she finally said, her voice barely above a discernible whisper.

I winced inwardly. I knew that Carrie had held on through Adam's drinking problem for years and now her loyalty was being repaid with her being kicked to the curb.

What a rotten deal.

"But that's not all," Carrie continued. "He said he's never really loved me. That I bore him and that's why he drinks. In fact, not only does he not love me, he loves someone else. And he's been cheating on me for years."

It was horrible hearing her words. And yet, I wondered if they were true. When I had tailed Adam, I'd never seen him with another woman. Was he just saying that? Coming up with an excuse to leave? Or was it true?

Ellen stood and went to Carrie, awkwardly putting her arm around her shoulder.

"It's going to be okay," she said.

Carrie slumped against my sister and stifled her sobs so her children couldn't hear her down the hall.

"I can't believe he's leaving me for...for..."

We waited.

Finally, she spit out the name.

"Judy fucking Platkin."

CHAPTER THIRTY-FIVE

Back outside, Ellen and I chatted while paramedics looked over Carrie Barnes.

"I've got an APB out on Adam," she said. "And Judy Platkin. I had my guys go over to her house. She's not home."

"I know where they are," I said.

"Oh, really," Ellen said, skepticism heavy in her voice.

"Well, I know the general area. Remember the warehouse I told you about?" I said. "And the sex club? I'm almost positive that's where they went. I just don't know the exact location and its entrance. I think it's hidden, or disguised somehow. Can you track Adam's cell phone?"

Ellen's face made an unhappy expression, which was pretty much a permanent condition.

"Sure, but that will take some time," she said.

"Hey, we're up," I said. "I feel like shit. I know you ordinarily need fifteen hours of sleep every night, but why not make an exception and head down to the warehouse district with me?" I said.

Someone had handed me a bottled water and some

Tylenol, so I took those and chugged the cold water. It tasted wonderful.

"And drive around in the dark with no idea of where we're going?" she asked. She checked her watch. "I've got a shooter on the run, a mess on Kercheval, and this," she said, gesturing at the scene outside the Barnes' household.

One of the extra cop cars pulled away from the Barnes' driveway and Ellen nodded to him as he passed us.

"You're the Chief of Police, aren't you?" I asked. "Can't you chase down this lead with me? You're the boss, right? Who's going to complain?"

"Oh believe me, someone will complain." I knew what she was saying. Being a female police chief made her a constant target of some of the Neanderthal elements in the department. They were always waiting for her to slip up.

"Look, it won't take long," I said. "Let's go downtown, I'll buy you a coffee on the way."

Ellen sighed.

"This seems like a really bad idea."

Without waiting, I opened the front door of her squad car and hopped into the passenger seat.

"I ought to put you in back," she said, as she slid behind the wheel.

We retraced my route down Jefferson and minutes later, found ourselves outside the abandoned warehouse.

"So this is it," she said. We were moving at a slow crawl around the perimeter of the building. Most of the streetlights in the area were long gone, most of them shooting victims. Target practice on streetlights was a favorite hobby of gun enthusiasts in Detroit. Plus, if you were a thief looking to assault and rob someone, complete darkness was your friend.

"What the hell was your buddy doing down here?" she asked.

Great question, I thought.

Ellen used the spotlight mounted above her side view mirror to illuminate all of the nooks and crannies of the warehouse.

Nothing.

"This is a real swinging place, John," she said.

"I don't think this is it," I replied. "But we're close."

"Close only counts in horseshoes and something else."

"I think it's herpes. Close counts in herpes."

Ellen let out a tired sigh.

"I'm just going to keep driving around but if this is all you've got," Ellen said, "you owe me breakfast."

We did another circle around the warehouse, then went on to the next abandoned building. It looked like it had once been a brick factory, at least according to faded paint on the exterior that had to be at least sixty years old.

"This must have been some place back in the day," Ellen said. "All the bootleggers coming over from Canada. The Purple Gang. Good times."

Another, smaller building painted a dark red had a metal sign with letters missing that had probably read Old Star Yeast. Most likely they had been suppliers to some of the distilleries that had cropped up when whiskey was in high demand.

We turned onto the next street and there was nothing but empty fields piled with rubble.

"I think you owe me—"

"Wait a minute," I said. Something had been triggered in my partially addled brain. "Go back. To the yeast place."

Ellen did a u-turn and slowly prowled past the dark red structure.

"If you're looking for a bagel, I think you're out of luck," Ellen said. But she slowed to a stop near the metal sign.

"What," she said. Not a question. A statement.

I looked up at the sign *Old Star Yeast*. The problem was the 's' was missing. So it actually read Old Star Yea_t.

And then I realized it was missing the first letter. A 'g.'

Gold Star Yeast.

And the sign was above the building's main entrance. A single door next to a wide window that had a metal covering.

It popped into my mind.

One of the chat rooms in the online sex club.

Gold Back Door.

"This has to be it," I said to Ellen. I filled her in on my theory and we both got out of the car. Ellen locked it, went to the trunk and pulled out a large pry bar.

"I need some probable cause," she said. "I'm not sure the name of a chat room in an online sex club is enough."

"I can say I saw Judy Platkin enter this building a couple nights ago, now that she's a known associate of someone you're searching for," I offered.

"That's what I was thinking," Ellen said. She glanced at the door.

"Ah," she said. "See the camera?"

Peering into the dark, I caught the tiniest reflection of a lens, above the door, pointing down. But I knew a lot of those had extremely wide ranges of view.

Ellen stayed far away from the door and then came up to the edge of the doorway from the side. I followed behind her. She held the pry bar with its pointed end up in her left hand and with her right she steadied herself against the wall.

"Boost me up," she said.

I laced my fingers together and she stepped into it, and then I lifted.

Something cracked and I assumed it was my vertebrae even though I had used proper lifting technique – with the legs not the back.

Glass tinkled onto the concrete and I knew the little

camera was out of commission, thanks to the working end of Ellen's pry bar.

The door was metal, as was the frame, but the metal flange covering the latch was thin and Ellen was able to pry it back, exposing the innards of the door mechanism. She adjusted her angle, leaned against the bar, and then motioned me to join her. Together, we heaved against the pry bar and the door broke free.

It swung outward and I instantly smelled a chemical odor and in the distance, heard a buzzing sound.

My sister went first and I followed closely behind.

Hey, she was the one with a gun.

CHAPTER THIRTY-SIX

For a sex club, it seemed to lack, shall we say, a certain ambiance. All of my favorite sex clubs were usually very plush.

A concrete landing led to a set of concrete steps with a rusted black metal handrail. Very industrial, very unfriendly feeling.

Ellen went up the stairs, which led to another landing and another set of stairs. Finally, the stairs stopped in front of an accordion-style door with a giant padlock. But the padlock was open.

The buzzing sound suddenly stopped and we could hear voices. It sounded like someone arguing.

Ellen slid her handgun from its holster and held it in front of her, pointed toward the ground.

She tilted her chin at the door and I slid the padlock from its slot. I grabbed both handles of the accordion door and held my breath.

This was going to be noisy.

With a heave, I wrenched the doors apart and the metal banged and crashed as Ellen darted through the opening. I followed her into a wide, expansive room with several stainless steel tables, a single harsh overhead light and a door to the left that suddenly banged shut.

Ellen ran across the room to the door and flung it open, then peeked around the corner.

A gun blasted and echoed throughout the room as Ellen ducked back around the corner.

"Shotgun," she said. She keyed the mike on her shoulder and asked for backup.

I felt fairly useless. All I had was the pry bar she'd handed me, so I glanced around to make sure someone wasn't sneaking up on us and I could clobber them.

Ellen peeked around the corner again.

"It's clear," she said and disappeared into the room.

I followed her and was aghast at what I saw.

A body on a stainless steel table was in the process of being dismembered, and Barry Kemp was on the floor with a hole in his chest and blood pooling out from beneath him in a widening circle of crimson. The wall behind the table was covered with surgical instruments. Several large coolers and bags of dry ice were spread out on the floor around the stainless steel table.

Barry Kemp was dead. This time there was no doubt. I looked closely at his body and at first I thought his hands were bloody but they were actually encased in surgical gloves, and those were covered in blood.

It appeared Dr. Kemp had been taking apart a body.

"Freeze!" Ellen shouted.

I looked over and Adam Barnes and Judy Platkin were standing in front of an open door that was a shallow closet, full of mops and brooms and assorted cleaning supplies.

Ellen advanced on them and I heard a rustle of feet from behind me and I swung blindly, the pry bar out in front of me and I rotated, swinging it in a backhand motion until I felt the heavy clunk of contact and a shotgun roared.

I felt a burning pain on the back of my left calf as it flew out from underneath me and I fell onto my side, coming face to face on the floor with a man I instantly recognized.

Carrot Top.

CHAPTER THIRTY-SEVEN

"Ellen!" I shouted, as I felt blood running down my calf into my sock.

Carrot Top, the redhead I'd sort of met in the office of the lawyer Gadlicke, was sound asleep on the concrete floor with a huge gash and lump on the side of his head from my expertly swung backhand.

It made me want to take up tennis again.

He was out for the count and I stared at his face. Who was this guy and why did he look familiar?

I rolled onto my stomach and pushed myself up until I was standing, a bit unsteadily, looking down at Carrot Top.

Across the room, I saw Ellen had Adam Barnes and Judy Platkin in handcuffs.

I limped over and nodded toward Ellen. "Did she put those cuffs on you or did you already have them on?" I asked the pair.

"Very funny," Judy said. She looked pale and disheveled. Adam looked like he was coming off a bad drunk.

Ellen had placed the handcuffs around the leg of a steel

table that was bolted to the floor. They weren't going anywhere.

She had left them, checked on Carrot Top, and was now opening something.

"John, look what's in the fridge," Ellen said.

I walked over to her and saw she was standing in front of an industrial-sized, double-door refrigeration unit big enough for two people. I say that, because it looked like there were parts of two people stuffed inside. I saw human organs, brains, hearts, and eyeballs. It looked like a serial killer's trophy room.

"Black market body parts," Ellen said.

Suddenly, realization slammed into my thoughts.

"Nate's serial killer," I said. Ellen looked at me.

"Nate's been covering a story about homeless people and hookers being murdered in Detroit, cut into pieces," I explained. "Nearly all of them infected with AIDS."

"Ah, that's a no-no," Ellen said. "There were rumors of a black market organ ring going around. Looks like someone decided it was easier to kill people for their parts than to harvest them correctly. My guess is they didn't tell their customers that the parts were infected."

"Kemp was mixed up in it," I said. "I bet Dave found out, or at least had an inkling." Suddenly, Carrot Top's face merged with Barry Kemp's. I remembered how Barry's gray hair was tinged with red. "Holy shit – they're brothers," I said to Ellen. "Barry Kemp and Carrot Top. And one or both of the Kemp boys killed Dave to keep the business going. Probably that piece of shit I knocked out with the pry bar. He killed his own brother," I said, realizing the scheme as it fell into place. "He and Gadlicke, they must have been black-mailing Barry into doing their dirty work for them. That's why Barry called me, and then Gadlicke and Carrot Top kidnapped him, but tried to make it look like he was dead."

Ellen closed the Refrigerator From Hell and turned back to me.

I held up a hand, "I know, I need to get out of here, back out on the street and act dumb."

"A role you were born for."

"But I want to see the sex club first," I said. I walked over to Adam Barnes and Judy Platkin.

"How do you get into the other place?" I asked. "They're going to find out how, you might as well tell us first."

"Fuck you," Adam Barnes slurred.

"Over there," Judy Platkin said. "But it's empty." She pointed to another accordion-style door. I went over and opened it. The lights were on and it looked like a medieval Hollywood set. Leather restraints. Benches. Some kind of pulley system and a wall full of dildos, whips and leather masks.

After asking Ellen to separate Adam Barnes and Judy Platkin, I formulated my theory to Judy. "This was all about Barry Kemp, wasn't it?"

"Yes, he was the Grand Master," Judy said. I knew that Barry had somehow arranged to pin that email address to Dave. Probably after Dave had started to find out what was going on. But Barry had sex pervert written all over him. The weightlifting, the obvious narcissism."

"So Gadlicke was blackmailing you?" I asked. It was mostly an educated guess, but I figured I was right.

"That bastard," she said. "It's why Adam started drinking so heavily. He was under so much pressure to pay off Gadlicke and hide the affair. It's why my husband left me," she said, and she began to weep. "I robbed his 401(k) to keep it quiet. He never really knew, but that was it for him. He never wanted to see me again."

"And Dave?" I asked.

She shook her head. "He was never here, but I think he found out what Barry was up to."

Ellen appeared and gave me a head-jerk.

It was time for me to go.

I walked out of the sex club/body part factory and found myself back on the street, leaning against the front fender of Ellen's squad car. The sun was just starting to come up and the first rays of light were hitting the Detroit River. Across the water, Canada still looked sound asleep, but here, more cop cars had arrived along with crime scene techs.

Another murderous morning in Detroit.

I picked up the phone and called my wife.

Suddenly, I wanted to talk to someone I loved.

Someone normal.

ALSO BY DAN AMES

DEAD WOOD (John Rockne Mystery #1)

HARD ROCK (John Rockne Mystery #2)

COLD JADE (John Rockne Mystery #3)

LONG SHOT (John Rockne Mystery #4)

EASY PREY (John Rockne Mystery #5)

BODY BLOW (John Rockne Mystery #6)

THE KILLING LEAGUE (Wallace Mack Thriller #1)

THE MURDER STORE (Wallace Mack Thriller #2)

FINDERS KILLERS (Wallace Mack Thriller #3)

DEATH BY SARCASM (Mary Cooper Mystery #1)

MURDER WITH SARCASTIC INTENT (Mary Cooper
Mystery #2)

GROSS SARCASTIC HOMICIDE (Mary Cooper Mystery #3)

KILLER GROOVE (Rockne & Cooper Mystery #1)

BEER MONEY (Burr Ashland Mystery #1)

THE CIRCUIT RIDER (Circuit Rider #1)

KILLER'S DRAW (Circuit Rider #2)

TO FIND A MOUNTAIN (A WWII Thriller)

STANDALONE THRILLERS:

THE RECRUITER
KILLING THE RAT
HEAD SHOT
THE BUTCHER

BOX SETS:

AMES TO KILL
GROSSE POINTE PULP
GROSSE POINTE PULP 2
TOTAL SARCASM
WALLACE MACK THRILLER COLLECTION

SHORT STORIES:

THE GARBAGE COLLECTOR
BULLET RIVER
SCHOOL GIRL
HANGING CURVE
SCALE OF JUSTICE

AFTERWORD

Do you want more killer crime fiction, along with the chance to win free books? Then sign up for the DAN AMES READER GROUP at

AuthorDanAmes.com

THE JACK REACHER CASES

A USA TODAY BESTSELLING BOOK

ON SALE NOW!

ABOUT THE AUTHOR

Dan Ames is USA TODAY bestselling author and winner of the Independent Book Award for Crime Fiction.

www.authordanames.com
dan@authordanames.com